Beverly Hills Prep

TANGLED
UP

SHANNON LAYNE

EPIC Escape

An Imprint of EPIC Press
abdopublishing.com

Tangled Up
Beverly Hills Prep: Book #5

abdopublishing.com

Published by EPIC Press, a division of ABDO, PO Box 398166, Minneapolis, Minnesota
55439. Copyright © 2019 by Abdo Consulting Group, Inc. International copyrights reserved
in all countries. No part of this book may be reproduced in any form without written
permission from the publisher. Escape™ is a trademark and logo of EPIC Press.

Printed in the United States of America, North Mankato, Minnesota.
052018
092018

Cover design by Laura Mitchell
Edited by Ryan Hume

Library of Congress Cataloging-in-Publication Data

Library of Congress Control Number: 2016962592

Publisher's Cataloging in Publication Data

Names: Layne, Shannon, author.
Title: Tangled up/ by Shannon Layne
Description: Minneapolis, MN : EPIC Press, 2019 | Series: Beverly hills prep; #5
Summary: Margot is a junior at Beverly Hills Prep, who is entangled with a group of girls who
    sell designer handbags to their classmates at a highly discounted rate. Eventually Margot
    ends up in trouble, with her grades dropping, and her dad seeing someone new, everything
    is falling apart. Can she figure things out with her family—and with school—or will she
    have to start over?
Identifiers: ISBN 9781680767124 (lib. bdg.) | ISBN 9781680767681 (ebook)
Subjects: LCSH: Family problems--Fiction. | Young offenders--Fiction. | Private
    preparatory schools--Fiction. | Teenage girls--Fiction | Young adult fiction.
Classification: DDC [FIC]--dc23

For any girl who's ever messed up, and needed to hear that it was all going to be okay.

*Oh, what a tangled web we weave,
when first we practice to deceive!*

—Walter Scott, from the poem *Marmion*

Chapter One

"I understand, Headmistress."

Margot gazed up at Headmistress Chambers through thick lashes, blinking her dark brown eyes innocently as a fawn. She was comfortable here in the headmistress's office—more comfortable than Chambers would like, she was sure of that.

"Do you, Ms. McKittrick?"

"I said I did," said Margot, rolling her eyes. She crossed one leg over the other. Her waistband was rolled just to make sure the uniform was a few inches too short; it drove the teachers insane to have to remind her every single day what the hemline regulations were, and she enjoyed that.

"You said it, but that doesn't mean I necessarily believe you."

Margot arched her brow at the headmistress, who sat implacable in her high-backed leather chair that looked more like a throne than a piece of office furniture. The headmistress was about as impenetrable as a block of ice—usually when Margot looked an adult directly in the eyes like this they would eventually cave and look away. Not Headmistress Chambers. The woman was like a glacier.

"What do you mean?" said Margot, innocently batting her lashes.

"When a professor has to come to me for grade reporting, Ms. McKittrick, that's not a good sign. If you would've shown up to the tutoring sessions arranged for your Calculus classes, we wouldn't be sitting here."

"They interfered with my personal life."

"I'm sorry to have to remind you that your

personal life comes second to your grades. You're now a student here on a partial scholarship, Ms. McKittrick. You can't afford for your grades to slip."

Thanks a lot for the reminder, Headmistress. I almost let myself forget.

"I'm aware of that, Headmistress," said Margot. "My grades are fine; I have a 4.0, for goodness' sake."

"Then what concerns me most isn't your grades themselves, but rather the fact that you've either been tardy or have skipped class completely six times in the past three weeks."

"Hey, I was sick at least one of those times."

"Margot, that's not acceptable. I know you're smart. That much has been established—but just because you continue to pass tests doesn't mean you're excused from showing up to class."

"Isn't that exactly what college is like?" said Margot. "You don't have to even step into a lecture if you're smart enough to pass the exams?"

"College classes are different than high school.

You aren't in college yet. You have nearly another two full years here with us before that will occur."

"But isn't that what you're supposed to be doing, anyway? Preparing me for college?"

The headmistress sighed, and Margot folded her hands serenely.

"I will say, I'm sincerely hopeful that you pursue a career in law after you graduate here, Ms. McKittrick."

"Ugh, never. Lawyers are spineless little cretins."

I should know, thought Margot. *I had to deal with enough of them during the divorce.*

The headmistress sighed again, but didn't respond.

"I expect you to attend the next of your scheduled makeup sessions for that class, Margot. And if I have to bring you in again for skipping, there will be consequences. Is that understood?"

"Yes, ma'am."

"Very well. Let's leave it at that, then. You may go."

"Finally," muttered Margot, rising to her feet.

"What was that?"

"I said, have a nice day," said Margot, smiling at the headmistress, and then she was free.

What was it about teachers anyway, huh? Margot thought to herself as she crossed campus. It seemed like all they really did was crush the spirits of girls like her and boss her around all the time. *Weren't they supposed to be teaching her something she didn't already know?* She knew that she was supposed to show up on time. She knew that she was supposed to turn her homework in and sit quietly during class and take notes. She also knew that she didn't care about any of those things.

Half of the girls in her class had fluff where their brains were supposed to be. Even the teachers' hardest tests weren't that difficult if you memorized what you were supposed to memorize. Margot didn't really understand a scrap of Calculus, not when it really came down to it. Without the formula, Margot couldn't tell the difference between anything on the paper anyway. But memorizing was something she could do.

Margot saw the world in pictures that she could flip through one at a time, like an enormous photo album of her life. It wasn't perfect, which she considered a rip-off. She'd heard of some people who had actual photographic memories and could remember every detail of anything they wanted. Margot's wasn't so perfect. She didn't even have an exceptionally high IQ, nothing like the weirdly smart girl who was a second year, Nora. That girl was always studying. Margot never studied—she just stared at the diagrams in books until she could pull them up in her mind. Sometimes she got them a little wrong, but most of the time it worked. The only problem was that all the tests she passed didn't make any sense to her without the diagrams and notes she'd memorized. That wasn't something Margot was concerned about, though. Would she really need any of this stuff later in life anyway?

Margot shivered in the chill of the air as she

walked back to her dorm room, nibbling at the cuticle of her thumb as she considered the headmistress's words. It would probably be a good idea to show up to the next few sessions she had lined up, just to get the woman off her back. As Margot walked across campus, she tangled her hands in the scarf around her neck to keep her fingers warm. There was a breeze blowing tonight that was chilly. If Margot could live in burning hot temperatures at all times, she would.

She'd lived in Arizona when she was younger, before the divorce, and she missed it even though they'd left when she was barely a teenager. If she closed her eyes she could still feel the heat on her cheeks from tilting her head up to the sun, the suffocating warmth radiating from the earth as the sun baked itself into the desert ground. As soon as she caught herself remembering, Margot mentally shook off the image, letting it fade from her mind like a bad dream. There was no point in thinking about those times—it just made reality more difficult to deal with.

Chapter Two

The Meadows dormitory was sprawled between the arboretum and the tennis courts, surrounded by enormous maple and oak trees that looked more suited to the English countryside than one of the most populated areas of the state. *They do a good job of making us forget where we really are,* Margot thought. *Almost, at least.* Not that being here was the worst thing in the world; Margot knew she would rather be here than at her dad's new condo in San Francisco, or at her mom's new house in New Mexico. Not that her mom had invited her to visit, anyway. Beverly Hills Prep might be nothing more than a very fancy, very expensive prison to Margot at times, but it was the best place she could be right now.

Margot opened the double doors and rubbed her shoulders as she stepped inside the halls, savoring the warmth. Pushing her hair back from her forehead, she took a sharp left and practically scurried down the hallway so she wouldn't have to talk to anyone. All she wanted to do was get inside her room and go to sleep. Never mind the fact that it was barely seven o'clock in the evening, apparently the only slot the headmistress had open; arguing with that woman was enough to make her need to stay in bed for a full week.

Margot fished out her dorm key from her backpack, cursing as she dropped it twice. Finally, she got the lock open and darted inside, leaning back against the door with a sigh of comfort, eyes closed, as it shut.

"Hard day?" she heard, and Margot opened her eyes.

"Oh, my gosh."

The common room was covered in either sheets of plastic tarp or white canvases. Some were splashed with color, countless others were smudged black and white, with charcoal. They all combined to create an enormous palette that Margot's roommate, Ophelia, was currently working on with a paintbrush in one hand, pushing her hair back from her face with the other.

"Sorry, I know it's a bit messy right now," said Ophelia apologetically, glancing from Margot's face back to her masterpiece.

"A bit?"

"I'll clean it up, I swear."

Margot shrugged.

"I don't mind the mess. You could leave it like this forever for all I care. It's the prefects who care if all our linens are in a row in our little drawers, not me."

Ophelia laughed, adding a streak of red to a canvas that looked like a row of very abstract daffodils. Margot cleared a space on the couch and plopped down with a sigh. Ophelia probably didn't even need to worry about prefects or marks on her records from failed room inspections; her grandmother was Lenore Koroleva, a direct descendant of the Romanov family. *Ophelia is literally descended from royalty,* Margot thought, *and my ancestors were indentured servants.*

The Koroleva line was rumored to have a family fortune in the billions, and they certainly lived like it, but Ophelia was as normal as a long-lost princess could be, at least to Margot. It wasn't her fault that her family was ancient Russian nobility. And it did have its perks, at least it seemed like it did— the only reason she was sharing a suite with Margot was because all the individual suites were gone by the time she transferred, and Beverly Hills Prep was surprisingly strict on reassigning living quarters.

Ophelia's family had donated a huge amount of money to the school—to get her in, presumably, though Margot wasn't sure why that was necessary.

What could Ophelia have done that was so bad? Whatever it was, they were naming the new west wing, and apparently a couple other buildings too, after her family. Ophelia was well known by every single person in the school. The prefects wouldn't come near her to discipline her. They were too afraid. The faculty treated her like she was some sort of prodigy, always asking her questions—mostly about whether or not her family had any other blood ties to this ancient prince or that long-dead duchess, or what it was like to have the last portrait ever painted of the Russian royals in her grandmother's family vault. It looked exhausting to Margot, and pretty boring.

"How'd your talk with the headmistress go?" asked Ophelia, slapping paint on a canvas.

"Fine, I guess," Margot said. "She didn't say anything I didn't already know."

"That sounds like a relatively good thing."

"It could've gone worse. She could've suspended me, or called my parents."

"Speaking of which, when was the last time you called them?"

Margot shrugged her skinny shoulders.

"We're supposed to go home for Christmas break in like a week, Marg. Don't you need to make sure they're going to pick you up from the airport or something?"

"I'll call my dad," said Margot. "I'll probably barely see him, anyway."

"What about your mom?"

Margot didn't talk about her mom. Her parents' divorce was pretty much public knowledge, since her dad was a prominent lawyer in the Bay Area (divorce mostly, which Margot found laughably ironic), and it had been an especially nasty one. Her parents had always argued a lot, ever since Margot could remember, but it had gotten steadily worse over the years. By the time her mom had filed for divorce, she was barely speaking to Margot, either. Instead, she'd walked around like a zombie, crying often, and saying little. Then, she'd packed, moved out, and was gone before Margot had realized what was happening. Margot had called her mom's cell phone over and over in the months following, but there'd been no response. All her dad would tell her was that her mom was living in New Mexico, and had asked him not to contact her for a while—except to make alimony payments, of course.

Before they broke up, her parents had plenty with her dad's salary to afford for Margot to go to Beverly Hills Prep on their own dime. But after the divorce, all that money got tied up in settlement and process fees, and Margot had gone on a partial scholarship so that her dad could also afford to support her mom. Her mom had basically no income of her own, and as far as Margot had heard, hadn't gotten a job. Her mom's employment was a hotly contested portion of the arguments. She didn't want to work, and Margot's dad didn't want to pay to support her. It was a never-ending, miserable process. The only thing that could've made it worse was a custody battle, but that didn't even enter her mom's mind, apparently. She'd signed off on letting Margot's dad have the majority of custody without batting an eye—not that it mattered too much, since Margot would be eighteen soon, and able to choose what she wanted to do. The entire subject wasn't something Margot liked to dwell on. It had been hard enough to go through it once—why relive it over and over again in her head?

"I'm going to shower and go to bed," said Margot, standing up from the couch and edging her way around one of Ophelia's canvases. "I haven't asked yet, but is this for a project or something, by the way?"

"You thought I would just do this for fun?"

"I don't know you that well, yet," said Margot, grinning, and it was true. Ophelia was a third-year transfer, so she'd only been at Beverly Hills Preparatory Academy for a few months since the start of the school year. Margot liked her a lot better than her old roommate, who had done nothing but gossip to her best friend, who attended a different private school, on the phone every night.

❧

Swinging her backpack onto her bed, Margot followed it and collapsed onto the sheets with a sigh. She locked her hands behind her head and took a deep breath. Margot figured the best description for her room was organized chaos, but minus the organized part. She shoved everything into the closet for inspections, or tried to—Beverly Hills Prep was so strict that the prefects still docked her points half the time because they opened her closet to check for clutter. Some were easier than others, but there was one that she swore was out to get her expelled based on demerits alone.

Margot's favorite color had always been the orange of a sunset, until someone told her how badly it clashed with her hair. Since then, she'd stuck to cactus greens and the dark blues of twilight skies she still remembered from Arizona. Sometimes she missed the orange, but it was true—her hair just wouldn't tolerate it. Everyone said that Margot had gotten her mother's hair and her father's temper. Her mom, on the other hand, had always been quiet, and more withdrawn from reality with the years. She was prone to bouts of melancholy that Margot had never understood, and when she was a kid, they'd terrified her. Her dad was more like Margot—loud and opinionated, according to some people at least.

Margot reached into her backpack and pulled out a book, rolling on her comforter, which was edged in turquoise in a Southwestern style. Her curtains were the standard ones doled out by the school, so they were a little lacy for her taste, but she made up for it with her favorite rug, which was embroidered with cactuses in chunky green thread. Ophelia couldn't even come into Margot's room without shuddering; apparently, for someone with actual aesthetic taste, her room was a horror scene. But Margot loved it. It made her feel like she was in a desert somewhere, and she even had real succulents and more cactuses lining the windowsill, facing toward the sun. California was great and all, and it was definitely sunny, but Margot wanted sand, and enough heat to bake a rattlesnake. Her mom used to say that Margot must be cold-blooded, like the lizards that sunned themselves on the rocks, and that was why she liked the heat so much.

Margot nudged off one of her flats, sighing with relief, and then heard the dull noise of her phone buzzing from within a pocket of her book bag. She dug it out and held it to her ear without checking the name.

"Hello?"

"Hey, Margot. It's Grace."

Margot's heart dropped into her stomach.

"Oh, hey."

Margot sat down onto her bed, suddenly very awake. Grace was always nice to her, but she was part of something that Margot had somehow become ensnarled in.

"Can you meet me in the Meadows parking lot?"

"Now?"

"Yeah."

"I mean, we're supposed to have Study Hall," Margot hedged. She'd been planning on skipping out on it but it sounded like a decent excuse.

"Find a way around it. It's not that hard; I manage it just fine."

There was a touch of impatience in Grace's voice now, and Margot didn't like the sound. She knew there was no point in fighting this.

"Fine. I'll get away and meet you in five minutes."

"Okay, but hurry."

"I will."

"See you then."

The line went dead.

Chapter Three

The prefect knocked on Margot and Ophelia's suite just as Margot finished stuffing some money into her backpack. She stood up from where she'd been kneeling, making sure none was left under her bed, and then swung her backpack onto her shoulders. She disliked doing this, but this was the last time. It had to be.

"I'm going to the library for Study Hall," Margot said to the prefect.

"Fine, just check in with the librarian."

"I'm going, too," said Ophelia, glancing at

Margot. She still had paint covering her hands up to her forearms.

"Whatever," sighed the prefect, checking her phone. Margot raised her eyebrows—this had to be the most lenient prefect she'd ever come into contact with. Maybe she was new. They all started to look the same to her after a while.

Ophelia locked their door behind her and Margot didn't wait for her, striding off instead in the direction of the parking lot.

"Margot, hold on."

"I'm late, Fi," Margot said, calling Ophelia by her nickname.

"For what, exactly?"

Margot kept walking down the hallway, but she turned to shoot a warning look at Ophelia tagging along at her side.

"You said you wouldn't say anything."

"And I won't. But Grace? Seriously?"

"She's nobody. She's just, I don't know. We're friends, sort of."

It was partially true. Grace herself wasn't anyone important; she was in their grade, but her family wasn't like Ophelia's. She wasn't the descendant of a queen, or something like a senator's daughter, but her family was still not one to be messed with. Grace had an older sister, who had since graduated, but in her time at Beverly Hills Prep she'd made an impression on Margot. She was the whole reason Margot was in this mess, really.

"She's mean to me," said Ophelia, and Margot's insides twisted. "She's mean to me and she's not exactly nice to you, either, and yet you keep doing exactly what she says."

"It's all temporary, I swear. Plus, what do you care if she's mean to you? From what I've heard you don't have much of an issue dealing with the people who are mean to you."

"I can't keep beating up everyone I hate," said Ophelia, so casually that Margot just stared. "I'm kidding. Really. Anyway, you've said that you'd stop doing whatever you're doing with Grace since the beginning of the year, but I still see you going to meet her."

"To be fair, we've only been in school for a couple of months."

"You know what I mean, Margot."

Ophelia stuck her arm across the corridor as Margot attempted to turn in the direction that would lead her to the parking lot instead of to the library.

"Don't do this," said Ophelia. "Promise me this is the last time."

"I'll try my best," said Margot. "I swear. Look, if not this time, then definitely the next time will be the last time I meet up with her."

Ophelia just stared at her, wisps of dark hair falling into her eyes. Margot didn't blink. She cared about Ophelia, and Grace was definitely a jerk, but she'd also been one of Margot's first friends at Beverly Hills Prep, and that wasn't easy to just forget. A part of Margot still wanted to impress Grace. It was a part she wasn't exactly proud of.

"I'm sorry she picks on you," said Margot. "Really."

"It's not that big of a deal," Ophelia said, sighing. "It's obnoxious, but I can handle it."

She moved out of the way so Margot could continue down the hallway.

"I'll cover for you at the library," said Ophelia. "Just please promise me you'll try and break things off with her, and soon. I don't know any details, but I know that whatever makes you guys meet up like this can't be a good thing for you."

"I swear I will," said Margot. "And thanks."

"No problem. I don't mind covering for you, Marg, but it can't last forever. You've got to choose. You know that, right? That Grace isn't that great a person to be around?"

"I get what you're saying," said Margot. "But everything is fine, okay? I'll see you tonight."

"Okay. See you later."

Ophelia smiled at Margot and turned to walk in

the opposite direction, entering the flow of traffic headed toward the library for Study Hall.

Margot smiled, but her hands went cold and there was a strange tightening inside her chest.

Chapter Four

Margot tried to banish Ophelia's comments from her mind as she continued toward the parking lot. Ophelia was definitely overreacting, though. Margot knew what she was doing—and the whole thing wasn't that big a deal.

Margot continued walking, taking corridors away from the rest of her classmates. She wasn't anywhere close to the library now, and if anyone asked where she was going she didn't have a good excuse in mind, but she knew how to avoid the prefects. Finally, Margot arrived at the side door that opened directly out to the parking lot and stepped through it, shifting her backpack on her shoulders.

Grace was waiting for her, over in the shadows near the now-empty parking lot. She wore her Beverly Hills Prep uniform just as Margot did, pleated skirt neatly ironed below the white button-up shirt, and navy vest. Margot, too, preferred the vest to the optional blazer.

As Margot approached her, Grace turned casually toward the east side of the building so they would be hidden from view. Margot walked to join her, feeling about as sneaky as a giant, flashing, neon-green Vegas sign. She was terrible at this part, the hiding and sneaking around. It seemed unnecessary, anyway— it's not like they were in the Secret Service, or doing something *really* bad.

Margot turned the corner of the building and found Grace waiting, her arms folded. She was a tall girl, built solidly—the fact that her name was Grace was like an ironic joke. She played on the water polo team and ran track, among her other extracurricular hobbies. Grace somehow always managed to look like she had a tan, and her hair was a light brown, almost blond but not quite, cut short around her shoulders. Her eyes were a brown hazel, and they tended to squint when she was annoyed.

"Hey, Margot. How's it going?" Grace asked, the way she always did, as though this was a totally chance meeting the two were having and that she hadn't just called to demand Margot meet her in a parking lot.

Margot glared at her, but shrugged. "It's going just peachy, Grace, thanks."

"Do you have everything?" said Grace, and Margot nodded. She opened her backpack for Grace, and Grace reached inside and pulled out the neat wad of bills. Grace flipped through them, glancing at Margot. "Doesn't seem like there's a lot here."

"I only had a couple of clutches this time, and that was it."

"Oh, that's right."

Grace scooped the cash easily into her backpack and Margot felt a little sick at what was coming.

"Look," Margot tried, stammering a little, "I told you guys that I don't want to do this, anymore. So why didn't anyone listen to me? I don't want to sell these designer purses anymore. I'm already in trouble with the headmistress for missing classes. I need to toe the line."

"This shouldn't interfere with your classes, Margot," said Grace, smiling. "I think you just need to work on your time management skills a little."

"You know what I'm trying to say," said Margot.

Grace rolled her eyes, looking bored.

"Margot," she said, "we've gone over this already. You've been doing this since last year. You know the drill. They know they can trust you to make the drops and not mess it up, except for that one time."

"Hey, that prefect was crazy; you know that wasn't my fault."

Margot didn't even like to think about what had happened earlier that year, when school had first started again in the fall; she'd gotten held up on the way to meet Grace, and when she'd finally gotten into the parking lot Grace had been stony and cold, a cell phone in her hand. While Margot had been in the middle of explaining what had happened, Grace told her she'd seen a glimpse through a window of Margot talking to a prefect and thought she'd been coming clean about the operation. Grace had canceled the call she'd made, whatever call that was, but Margot had seen the look on her face and knew whatever would've happened to her wouldn't have been pleasant.

Until that point, Margot hadn't realized the whole operation was so important. To her, it was just a fun way to make some extra money. It hadn't seemed like a big deal at the time. And when Margot had gone on a partial scholarship, the extra money helped her pretend she was still normal. The pocket money made her feel like less of a charity case.

"Exactly," said Grace. "You're good at this, for the most part. Can't you just keep doing what you're doing? We are paying you, after all. It's not that big a deal to keep doing it a little longer."

"I don't need the money," denied Margot. It was easier to pretend than to admit that her family wasn't exactly swimming in cash at the moment.

"Do you want a free bag or something? We have a nice Louis Vuitton in right now." Margot raised her eyebrows as Grace grinned at her.

"I don't want it," said Margot. "What I want is to stop being your distributor, or whatever you want to call me. I don't want to deliver these bags to the girls who order them anymore. It's stupid."

Grace sighed.

"If you really want out that bad, I can try and work it out."

"This whole thing has just gotten out of hand," said Margot. "I hung out with you guys a couple times and somehow got roped into this. It started out as nothing but a joke, but it's not so funny now."

"I said I'll see what I can do," said Grace. "Relax.

Just deal with these little clutches and don't say anything until I see you again."

"I know the drill," grumbled Margot, as Grace stuffed a couple of designer clutches into her backpack. Grace looked around the corner of the building, making sure the coast was clear, and Margot resisted laughing. They acted like this was such a huge thing, and it really wasn't. Was it? Margot assumed that the purses, clutches, and handbags she sold were originally purchased legally. And that was fine, wasn't it? Margot wasn't sure of the logistics, but she wasn't that concerned.

"Wait," said Margot. "Also, I would appreciate it if you left my roommate alone."

"Who?" said Grace, still scanning the courtyard.

"Ophelia."

"Oh."

"Come on, Grace, please. She's never done anything to you."

"She thinks she's better than everyone here," snapped Grace. She cracked her knuckles ominously, and Margot thought idly that she looked a bit like an ogre. Not a super flattering look.

"She does not, and anyway, she sort of is," said Margot, attempting a joke. "She's royalty. The rest of us are just peasants."

Margot was just trying to make a joke, but Grace's eyes narrowed.

"Speak for yourself," said Grace coldly.

"Wow, okay. Fine," said Margot, stung. "Anyway, just keep in mind that it would be a nice favor to me if you wouldn't be so mean to her."

Grace sighed, and rolled her eyes.

"Fine. See you in two weeks," said Grace, and then she was gone, heading around the side of the building and back inside, the door slamming behind her.

Margot watched her walk away, blinking slowly and wondering how she'd ever thought Grace was one of her friends. This was all so messed up. Sighing, Margot brushed off her skirt and set off toward the door Grace had just entered. There was still plenty of time for her to meet Ophelia in the library for Study Hall. In the meantime, she'd try to forget the entirety of this very weird and uncomfortable conversation with someone Margot, at least sort of, considered a friend.

Chapter Five

Margot slipped into the library via the side door in the very back of the room, next to the bookshelves. She moved into the aisle, darted across the open space to the empty seat next to Ophelia, who was scribbling something in a notebook, and sat down.

"Hey," muttered Margot, sliding into the chair. "How's it going?"

"Just fine," Ophelia answered. "Just trying to study."

Margot opened her backpack, taking her books and a notebook out. Her laptop was in her room and she hadn't gotten permission to use it, anyway. Ophelia slipped headphones in her ears, and Margot followed suit, trying to let Merle Haggard soothe her nerves.

"You need to relax," muttered Ophelia, glancing at the librarian, who appeared to be snoozing in her chair, her glasses askew.

"What are you talking about?"

"You're radiating tension. Your back isn't even touching the chair. Chill out."

Margot sighed, rolling her pen up and down the lines of her notebook.

"I'm just wondering how I got myself into this situation."

"Well, did you get yourself out of it?"

"I tried," Margot protested. "I swear."

"Margot . . . " Ophelia trailed off, but the look she gave Margot was stern.

"I think it might happen soon, though," said Margot. "I told her I was going to stop and she said she'd pass it along."

"Marg, you know I like living with you," said Ophelia quietly.

"Sure. You're pretty cool, too."

And she was. Ophelia wasn't aloof and distant like the other popular girls; she listened to Margot when she was on a crazy *Gilmore Girls* rant, she shared her raspberry tarts when there weren't any left in the dining hall, and she didn't make Margot feel badly about her parents' divorce like everyone else did.

"But I can't keep living with you if you're going to keep doing this. At the beginning of the year it wasn't so bad, but now you keep going out to meet Grace on these weird errands. And you always told me you would stop."

Margot looked down at her hands, the cuticles bitten to shreds.

"You'd seriously request to change dorms?"

"Margot, I don't want to, but I'm hanging by a thread here. It took all the influence my grandma has to get me in here at all, with my record, and I can't mess it up. I can't afford to get tangled up in something like this."

"You're not doing anything," said Margot, lowering her voice to a whisper. "You're not involved. You've been well behaved the whole year."

"You know what I mean," said Ophelia. "I'm your roommate. It doesn't look good, if anything should happen and you got into trouble."

Just the thought gave Margot a sick feeling in the pit of her stomach.

"You're a Koroleva," Margot protested. "I think you have more sway than you think."

"You don't know my record," said Ophelia. "You don't know how hard it was to get in here at all."

"You're right, I guess," Margot admitted. She didn't know all the details of Ophelia's life before she'd arrived at Beverly Hills Prep. Ophelia wasn't especially chatty about her past, not that Margot blamed her. The two of them had that in common.

"I'm sorry."

The girls were quiet for a while, Margot doodling

pointlessly in her notebook and Ophelia taking notes from a presentation.

"You never really told me how you got started in whatever you're involved in, anyway," said Ophelia. "I don't want to know the details, just in case, but you're my friend, and I'll listen, if you want."

"It's not a very long story."

Margot leaned her head on her hand, scribbling aimlessly on her paper. She didn't want to talk about it, not even with Ophelia. It wasn't that it was such a terrible story, but thinking of it always made her feel stupid. Almost against her will, Margot's mind drifted, taking her back to the beginning of it all.

Chapter Six

When Margot first came to Beverly Hills Prep, as a starry-eyed freshman, she expected everything to come easily. This was pre-divorce, when her mom was still around, and her dad came home early from work just to be with them both. Margot had gone to a pretty average middle school, but by the time she was ready for high school her parents decided she needed to go somewhere more prestigious, somewhere that fit her new social status.

Her father wasn't slaving away at the firm anymore—he'd moved to partner, and her mom had quit her job as a secretary and was at home wearing silky robes and talking on the phone constantly to the other wives in the firm, who were suddenly interested in her now that she was a *partner's* wife. She took Margot shopping on school days and let her pick out anything she wanted, the new driver taking bags and bags from Nordstrom and Ralph Lauren and Gucci back to the car.

Margot had been completely intoxicated with their new life. Her parents seemed so happy, and when Margot went to orientation at Beverly Hills Preparatory Academy, she thought she'd never seen a place more beautiful. The grounds were pristine and sprawling, and the campus looked like something out of a postcard. The buildings were all brick and mortar, ivy-covered, and inside, everything was even more magical.

The marble floor of the foyer in the administrative building had been walked on by Robert Frost, and the heavy oak door was donated from President John Adams's home estate. There were massive crystal chandeliers imported from post-imperial Russia, curving staircases with hand-carved banisters, and there was even a letter from Edgar Allen Poe on display in one of the main corridors. It was like another world.

Margot—with her frizzy red hair and her childhood that had been so boring and normal compared to the girls who'd grown up on movie sets and spending their summers in French châteaux—was spellbound. On her first day as a freshman she was ready in her brand-new uniform, hand-pressed by her mom's new maid along with the rest of her skirts, vests, and crisp linen shirts. Her roommate at the time had been a transfer student from Austria, a timid and shy girl, and she'd barely spoken two words to Margot. Margot brushed it off, certain that her first days in school would bring new friends. She'd never had trouble making friends before; it came pretty easily to her, with her loud laugh and her natural tendency toward chattiness.

The other girls weren't what Margot expected.

She knew they'd be rich, and she knew they'd

come from families that had money long before her dad did, but who cared? They all showed up at the same place every single day, in the exact same uniform. Surely, the divide wasn't so great. And to Margot, it wasn't. But the other girls seemed to know that she was an outsider, and that she didn't belong. Margot was surrounded by girls who had been born into more money than she'd ever dreamed of, and they could somehow smell on Margot that she hadn't.

They talked about designers she'd never heard of, and places she'd never been, and they ignored Margot. It wasn't so much that they were mean— it was that they literally treated her as though she didn't exist, as though she was a mundane object, the same way they'd respond to a wall or a chair. Margot tried to be extra vivacious her freshman year, loud and bubbly, just in an effort to make some friends. By the time she left for the summer, she was near a breaking point. She cried as soon as she got home, and had seen her mother.

"No one likes me," Margot had sobbed into her mother's arms. "They all just ignore me. I have no friends."

She'd barely noticed the fact that her mom was too thin, that her smile was brittle and forced. Margot, caught up in her own problems, barely noticed that she wasn't the only one who was hurting. Margot thought back to that moment over and over again in the following days—if she would've paid more attention to her mom the times she saw her over the school year, could she have prevented what had happened? Maybe if she hadn't been so caught up in her own problems, her mom wouldn't have been so tired of her that she left without even telling Margot she was going.

"Margot, come on. We need to go back to our dorm."

"Huh? Oh, sorry."

Margot was jolted from her mental trip down memory lane by Ophelia nudging her shoulder.

"We're the last ones here," said Ophelia, stuffing books into her bag. "It's close to time for lights out."

"Alright, alright."

Margot grabbed her stuff absently, and followed Ophelia out of the library with a sigh. The magnificent arched walkways and the sheer vastness of the rows of bookcases always intimidated Margot, but Ophelia seemed to barely notice them. Margot understood by now that when you are raised in splendor, it becomes normal. Beverly Hills Prep would always be a sort of palace to her.

Even when she and her parents moved from their condo into the sprawling, multimillion-dollar townhouse with its view of the sea, Margot remembered their tiny house in Arizona. The new place was almost too open, with too much empty space. In their old house they'd been crammed together in the tiny rooms. While her mom had complained at the time that she wanted a bigger yard for her gardens, more space in the house to decorate and allow for breathing room, when they'd left it behind Margot found herself wishing they could go back. Now, of course, that larger house had been put on the market because of the divorce, for some other family to be unhappy in.

Margot couldn't change the fact that she wasn't used to money—she probably never would be, even now that she knew what it was like to have it. That was something she was fine with. Other girls sailed on yachts and went to celebrity weddings and acted like it was just a typical day, and Margot would never be able to understand that kind of normal. But it separated her from a lot of the other girls within the realm of Beverly Hills Prep.

There were a few girls who were here on scholarships and whatnot, girls who came from more average families, but most of them were weird, or at least totally antisocial. All Margot wanted was to be one of the normal ones, not one of the girls on the fringe of Beverly Hills Prep. Ophelia, on the other hand, couldn't care less, but she was in automatically because of her family. The whole setup was twisted.

"You're pretty quiet tonight," said Ophelia as they headed down the deserted hallway toward their room.

"Loud talking is discouraged in the library," said Margot.

"You know what I mean."

"I guess."

Ophelia unlocked the door with a twist of her wrist, glancing back at Margot.

"I'll have the paintings out of here by tomorrow, I swear."

"I told you, it's no big deal. Whenever is fine."

Ophelia smiled at Margot, squeezing her arm gently, and Margot caught herself thinking of how good a roommate Ophelia was. It would really suck to lose her.

"Are you ready for that Environmental Science quiz tomorrow?"

"No," sighed Margot. "I can't even think about looking over my notes for that thing."

"It's worth a ton of our grade."

"Perfect," said Margot sarcastically.

"Do you need help studying?"

"No, I should be okay. Thanks, though."

Margot rubbed a hand over her face; it wouldn't take long to look over her notes for the quiz, but she was exhausted. She couldn't fail this quiz, though—the headmistress would have a field day if her grades started to drop on top of her attendance issues. Margot chewed restlessly on a fingernail, wishing she had done more schoolwork during study hall so she could go to sleep now, or at least wishing she'd grabbed a soda from the dining hall to keep herself awake.

"Well, good night," said Ophelia. "See you in the morning."

"You, too," said Margot. She grabbed her backpack and walked into her bedroom, locking the door behind her. Her favorite pajamas with the cacti on them would be her choice tonight.

Margot sat down on her bed, tracing the embroidery with her fingertips. Outside her window there was nothing but darkness and the dim glow of one of the garden lights illuminating the path that led around the dormitory. It was quiet and still, and Margot yawned hugely, rubbing her eyes. She really did need to call her dad and make sure he knew when her holiday break was, or he might forget she was coming. Margot's mind flipped through all the things she needed to do the next day, the quizzes, and the stress of talking to her father, and she sighed. Sometimes it all seemed like too much stress for one person to deal with.

Chapter Seven

"Is that really all you're taking home?"

Margot looked down at her orange suitcase, the perfect carry-on size, and shrugged.

"Yeah, this is all I need. I travel a little lighter than you."

Ophelia shook her head, and Margot noticed she had what looked like four suitcases in her own pile. Ophelia, low maintenance in most respects, had more clothes than Margot had ever seen. Margot just couldn't see the point of stuffing a closet at school when they wore a uniform every single day. Margot had a no-nonsense black dress for events and a few pairs of jeans, and other than that she stuck to wearing comfortable T-shirts and leggings. Ophelia had clothes still hanging up with the tags on them. On the bright side, she was happy to let Margot borrow whatever she needed.

"Are you excited to go home?" Ophelia asked, trying to buckle the last strap on her biggest suitcase.

Margot didn't know how to answer that. She wasn't going home—not really. She was going to San Francisco to stay with her dad in his apartment, and then she was coming back here as soon as she possibly could. She wished that her mom was coming with her, and that she didn't have to spend the holiday alone at her dad's.

I need you, Mom, Margot wanted to say to her mother. *I need you, so I don't have to go to Dad's by myself and be alone.* Last year at this time, the divorce had been in progress, but her mom hadn't left yet. Her mom had tried to make the holiday somewhat festive, setting out extra presents and keeping the decorations up, but it had been completely hollow.

Everything was beginning to fall apart and they all knew it. The glass balls on the tree didn't make a real difference.

"I'll be excited when it's over," was all Margot said back to Ophelia. They hugged and then locked the door behind them, Margot dragging two of Ophelia's suitcases for her. The hallways were deserted and quiet, with just a few stragglers left behind. It was almost eerie, the lack of noise in the dormitories. Usually it was filled with chatter and the sound of footsteps. Now it was like it had been abandoned. It didn't brighten Margot's mood—that was for sure.

In the parking lot, Ophelia headed for the black Escalade her driver was waiting in, and Margot grabbed an Uber. As soon as she got in, she put her headphones in and turned the volume to blasting. Making polite chitchat with her driver wasn't something she had the energy for today.

Two hours later, Margot was in an airplane seat next to the window, idly tapping her fingers on the armrest while she waited for takeoff. It was a short flight to SFO, just a little over an hour, and she found herself wishing it were longer—anything to prolong the time before she had to see her father. When it was just the two of them, it was more difficult to act as though their lives were normal. All that had changed in the last year became even more apparent, and the harder they tried to act normal, the more obvious it was that everything was different. The dynamic of her family had completely changed when her parents separated. Margot was an only child, and sometimes she felt like it would be easier if she had a sibling to share the loneliness with. When her parents focused on her, they fought over which one of them she loved most. And when they ignored her, it was even worse.

Margot leaned her head back against her seat, letting her mind drift.

Margot had found herself thinking a lot about what Ophelia had asked her in the library—about how she'd gotten involved in this type of situation in the first place. It wasn't anything she dwelled on, but Ophelia's question had opened up the gates to a flood of memories she hadn't revisited in a long time.

Chapter Eight

Margot had gone into her second year at Beverly Hills Prep determined to have a completely different experience than she'd had as a freshman. Her naïveté was gone, replaced by a more cynical understanding of her place in the school. But she was still lonely. She wanted friends.

The first few months of the year dragged by. Margot's new roommate was a senator's daughter who perpetually ignored her and spent most of her time straightening her hair and complaining about the dress code. She wasn't Margot's favorite person in the school, but she had a variety of friends who came in and out of the dorm and Margot hoped that one of them, anyone, really, would realize that she was cool.

One Friday night, Margot had come home to her dorm room to hear her roommate talking excitedly with a group of seniors. None of them were dressed in uniform, and they all had makeup on and their hair done; Margot realized, with a jolt of jealousy, that they were probably going to a party somewhere. Margot recognized a few of the faces, but none of them had been girls she knew well.

"I'm totally down to go to the party," her roommate was saying. "But I don't want to bring any of the bags with us. The administration just had that tip that they were being sold on campus. What if we get checked before we leave the building? I could be expelled."

"It's not that big of a deal," one of the older girls had replied. "No one has gotten caught in a long time."

"Still, it's risky."

"Can't we just leave them here?"

"I told a bunch of girls I would bring some clutches and wallets for the whole party in case anyone wanted to buy one," said an older girl. "I can't just show up with nothing."

"Well, I don't want to be the one carrying it all out. They'll probably check our after-hour passes. Someone got suspended the last time, when they realized she had eight Chanel wallets stuffed into her backpack and they put the pieces together."

Margot had lingered in the doorway of her bedroom, listening to the conversation. Margot had never been to a party at Beverly Hills Prep. Come to think of it, she had never been invited by another girl to do anything over the weekend. Margot took a deep breath, and she stepped into the common room.

"I can carry the bags," she said.

For a moment, no one said anything. Her roommate glared at her, and then one of the older girls smiled.

"Are you sure?"

At this point, Margot didn't even know why everyone else was being so hesitant. It was just a few purses, after all. But what she did know was that she couldn't spend another Friday night alone in her room. So she nodded her head, smiled, and tried to look older than she was. Her roommate scowled, but the rest of the girls shrugged and seemed to accept it without issues.

"We're going to a party," said the older girl who'd smiled at Margot. "So you're going to need to change."

"Into what?" said Margot.

They ended up choosing her black dress, with black boots, and a jacket that she could use to sneak out the Yves Saint Laurent clutches and the Prada wallet. Margot could barely hold back her excitement as she got ready with the rest of the girls; she almost forgot that she was supposed to be carrying something until the same older girl approached her again.

"I'm Kara, by the way," she said, tossing dark hair

over her shoulder. "Thanks for doing this for us—we really owe you one."

She handed over the wallet and clutches, and Margot hesitated for a moment. Later, she would go back to that moment over and over again in her mind—what would have happened if she had said no, or walked away? What would have been different? How would her life have changed?

Margot thought of her lonely room, and her parents, who were now involved in a vicious war over things like who got the townhouse and who was going to take the Cadillac as opposed to the Jeep. It was miserable, and not having any friends certainly wasn't helping.

Margot took the merchandise and tucked it into her jacket. She had forged her mother's signature before, so forging it on an after-hours pass was easy. The rest of the girls grabbed coats and sweaters and they left the dorm room. The hallway was filled with other girls, some in sweatpants lounging against the wall and chatting with others, enjoying the Friday night release from the dress code, and some were dressed like them in fancier clothes. They were probably going out to dinner with boyfriends or parents, meeting someone who cared about them. *I don't have either of those things,* thought Margot. *I have nothing to lose.*

The resident faculty member stopped them at the exit of the dormitory, which was the standard procedure, to check their passes. Margot pulled hers out of her pocket and handed it over with a smile. She felt supremely confident—daring, even. She was going to a party. She didn't think it was possible to be more excited. Even the fact that she had only been invited because she was carrying the designer merchandise to be sold at the party didn't dim Margot's excitement. She'd been lonely for too long.

R

Kara was Grace's sister; that night had been the start of it all. Margot started being invited along to other parties with Kara and her friends. Sometimes she carried purses and such out of the dorm and sometimes she didn't, but she became a part of the group.

From there, everything had just spiraled. One weekend Kara had asked her to go to a party at a house she'd been to several times, and Margot said yes. Then Kara had said they had a Birkin bag left over from the party the weekend before; she asked Margot if she would mind finding someone who would buy it. The girls who attended Beverly Hills Prep shelled out the discounted prices for these bags with no problem. Most of them had multiple credit cards, or money dropped into their account anytime they asked. Margot didn't know enough about the process to know exactly how Kara and the other girls were making a profit off of selling the bags, but she didn't really want to know. It was better that she wasn't privy to all the details.

"Me?" said Margot. "Are you, um, sure?"

"It's not a big deal," Kara had said airily. "It was

the only one left over, and I just need to get rid of it. I assume you don't want it."

"For myself? No, I'm good," said Margot. She could never afford even the discounted price of a Birkin bag, but she didn't want to admit that.

"Then do you mind? It won't be that hard to find someone who will take it. Any of the girls we normally go out with will buy it, or one of their friends. It will really help me out."

Margot had hesitated, but in the end she agreed. It didn't seem like that big a deal—it was just finding someone to take the bag off Kara's hands. Margot was doing a friend a favor, and also making a cut of the cash in the process. It had seemed harmless enough.

But from that one instance had spiraled many other nights where Kara had asked for the same "favor." After a while, girls just started going straight to Margot for handbags, purses, clutches, wallets, and everything in between—which, as it turned out, was exactly what Kara had planned. It changed from the one-time to a few times a week, and then more and more. Margot felt uncomfortable doing it for a while, but she always just considered it a favor to Kara. Kara was the first girl in Beverly Hills Prep who'd even taken her to a party, and been nice to her.

Then Kara graduated, and Grace had been charged with partnering with Margot and keeping the whole process going. Now, Margot was running a show she'd never really wanted to be a part of in the first place, and every effort she made to escape just seemed to drag her deeper into the mess she'd made.

"Attention guests flying on flight 5754 into San Francisco: we are about to begin our descent. Please place your seats upright and close your tray tables in preparation for landing."

Margot put her headphones into her backpack and looked out the window; all she could see was a gray sky and the raindrops that slid against her window like tears. The sooner this stupid break could be over, the better. She wished she could actually look forward to seeing her dad without worrying about how awkward it was going to be. Part of her wished she could just disappear, instead, to someplace where things were simpler. If she were being honest, Margot would give anything to go back for one more day to the way things were before the divorce. It was easier to be at school. Things might not be perfect, but at least she could act like her family wasn't as dysfunctional as it was in reality. How could Christmas be Christmas when everything was so messed up?

Chapter Nine

When she exited the plane, Margot looked around for her father, but she didn't see his face in the crowd. Dragging her carry-on, Margot headed for the exit—maybe he was waiting at the arrivals area. Her phone buzzed in her hand, and Margot read the text while navigating her way through the crowds of SFO:

Busy at work. Charles will drive you to the house. Be there as soon as I can.

Perfect. Her own father couldn't be bothered to come and get her from the airport. This was a really nice start to her visit. Even though Christmas break lasted a full two weeks, Margot was only staying until the day after Christmas. It would be better to be on an empty campus alone than to overstay her welcome at her dad's. Things were so awkward between them right now, and he was working more than ever. Margot knew they had bills to pay, but it seemed like more of an excuse to ignore Margot than anything else. Margot rolled her eyes at the text and kept walking. At least she wouldn't have to pay for a cab all the way to her dad's place.

After two hours of sitting in traffic, Margot finally made it to her father's condo. It was a two-story brick building on the edge of the city. In the rain it looked cold and lonely. Margot let Charles carry her bags inside to the foyer and then upstairs; the condo was tiny, and it looked so much like a bachelor pad that it made Margot want to cry. There was a living room with a leather couch and a flat-screen

TV, and two small bedrooms. Margot's was sparsely decorated, but the mattress was soft and comfortable and there was a tiny desk. The place was quiet with just Margot inside. She plopped herself down on the leather couch and turned on the flat-screen TV, letting the noise drown out the silence.

Margot woke to the sound of the front door creaking open; then there was the noise of feet shuffling on the downstairs carpet. Margot frowned, checking her phone. It said it was close to midnight. *Was her dad really just getting home?*

Then a door slammed and he walked into the living room, still wearing his suit and tie from the office.

"Dad?"

He jumped at the sound of her voice, looking around wildly for the source of the sound.

"Margot! Jeez, you scared me half to death."

"It's nice to see you too, Dad."

He hugged her stiffly with one arm and Margot felt like he had to resist the urge to pat the top of her head.

"Are you always home this late?" said Margot, sitting back down on the couch. Her dad sat down on the armchair across from the couch, leaning awkwardly on the cushions. He unbuttoned his cuffs, and Margot thought he looked older than she'd remembered. He had less hair—that was for certain. But he had that same sharp look about him, the same direct gaze that Margot had learned from him.

"I get home earlier than this most nights."

Margot nodded. "So, how are things at the firm?"

"They're going just fine."

"Sent anyone to jail lately?"

"Surprisingly, the divorce court hasn't sent many people to prison as of recently," her father said wryly. "Did you make it here okay?"

"Charles is a very safe driver, yes."

"You look thin," said her father critically. "That sweater is baggy on you."

"I'm not too thin, Dad."

"Your cheekbones seem like they're sticking out more than usual."

"That coming from someone who looks like they've been burning the candle at both ends."

"What does that mean?"

"You didn't come home until midnight tonight. It just seems like you're really busy."

"Well, I am. Your mother's bills are through the roof. I've had to take on so many new clients to cover those expenses that I barely have time to be home."

"I really don't want to listen to you bash on Mom, Dad," Margot sighed.

"Fine. We don't have to talk about it. But just know that if she'd just get a job, this whole thing would be a lot easier."

"I don't want to hear this, Dad," snapped Margot. It was too hard, when her mom wouldn't even talk to her, to hear her dad talking about her.

"She did want me to tell you something," said her dad. "She said she's gotten your calls, and your letters, and she'll respond when she's ready."

Margot's dad turned to look at her, pity in his eyes. "You wrote her letters, Marg? I haven't seen a kid your age write a letter in years."

"Yeah, I did," Margot muttered. "I don't want to talk about it."

Her dad raised his hands in a gesture of surrender, and Margot crossed her arms over her chest.

It was like she was right back in the virtual nightmare of the divorce. The transition to partner had done something to her father. He started working longer hours, spending even more time at the office than he had before the promotion. The warm, humorous man who used to come home and hug Margot every single day, no matter how tired he was, had transformed into someone blunt and efficient, obsessed with the company's profits and executive decisions. It was always ironic to Margot that when he started making more money was when he became insanely dedicated to the business; she'd sort of assumed that when he finally hit his goal and became a partner that his working hours would become more flexible. But that wasn't the way it turned out at all.

Margot's mother had been isolated at the house, increasingly suspicious of her husband and his whereabouts. She went to functions and attended company events with her husband, and her closet became filled with sparkly dresses that Margot would try on whenever she could. There were more housekeeping staff hired and Margot's mom could afford to do things like get her hair and nails done, and that was what Margot's father encouraged her to do.

"Now that I'm finally a partner, I need your mother to look the part," he'd say to Margot while they waited for her mom to put the finishing touches on her makeup before an event. It seemed straightforward enough to Margot, but her mother started to crumble under the pressure.

Margot could remember her mom talking to her on the phone, the tightness in her voice when

Margot asked about her dad. Finally, the entire situation had spiraled out of control.

"Well, I'm headed to bed," said Margot's dad. "I'll see you in the morning, kiddo."

"Are you going to be here in the morning?"

She saw him hesitate.

"I'll need to be in the office a lot in the next few days," he hedged. "I have a ton of work to get done before Christmas Day."

"How much could you possibly have to do? Isn't everyone out of the office at this time of year anyway?"

"Yeah, Margot, they are, which means there's a lot of slack for me to pick up. The senior partners have a lot more leeway with that kind of thing than I do."

"Okay."

There was a moment of quiet, and Margot ran a hand through her hair, crossing her legs on the couch.

"I'll be home as much as I can," said her dad finally. "I promise."

"It's fine," Margot lied. "But it would be cool to not have to be here the entire time by myself."

"Understood. Now, I'm going to bed. I suggest you do the same—it's late."

"Alright, fine. Good night."

"Good night."

He eased himself off the edge of the chair and headed to the master bedroom. Margot heard the shower start and she leaned back into the couch cushions with a sigh. This was going to be a very merry Christmas—she could already tell.

Chapter Ten

The next couple of days were more peaceful, admittedly, than Margot had expected. Her dad spent most of the day at the office, coming home late at night and leaving again the next morning, usually before Margot was up. She got used to staying up late with the TV on, falling asleep on the couch, and then waking up and moving to her bed in the other room when her dad came in. One morning she woke up to find herself still on the couch with a blanket over her; that was nice of him, at least.

It poured the entire time that she was there—great, heavy sheets of rain that turned the skyline a permanent shade of sleet gray. Margot texted her dad the first day that he was gone, and called the office, but there was no answer. Her bitterness spread like a chill in her bones. She had come home for the holidays, but all she was doing was sitting alone on the couch. If her dad really hadn't wanted her here he should have let her stay at school.

Margot was under the couch blanket the day before Christmas, flipping idly through the channels and debating whether or not she should order takeout. She dialed the number for the Chinese place down the street. Some pot stickers sounded good.

Her dad still hadn't come home by dinnertime, despite Margot's calls, so she ate the rest of the leftovers and grabbed a book from the bookshelf. She watched the light change from sunset to starry through the layer of fog, and then the next thing she knew she was jolted awake by the sound of voices. The room was dark, except for the TV, which was murmuring at a low volume. Margot sat up, hidden against the back of the couch when she heard the voices again. She recognized the low chuckle as her father, and her hands clenched in the blankets when a softer one answered him.

Margot stood up slowly, letting the blanket drop silently to the floor. It sounded like they were still in the stairwell. One foot at a time, Margot edged her way from the couch to the landing above the stairs, where she'd have a full view of the front door. With every step she listened to her dad's voice mingling with what she was now sure was a woman's voice. Margot was pulled toward the noise almost against her will; she didn't want to see what was going on at the front door, but she couldn't stop herself from walking toward the sound. Something in her just had to see it.

Margot leaned over the rail slowly, staying in the shadows, and her father came into view. He was standing next to a woman in the stairwell, someone with dark hair, and her smile flashed in the dim light. Margot thought she was going to be sick.

Images flashed through Margot's mind of her

mom and dad dancing in the living room in each other's arms—of her dad coming home and kissing her on the cheek every single day—of him telling her he loved her while she sat next to him on the couch. *How could he do this? He'd traded her in, traded them both in, for an entirely new life.*

Margot stood like that for a while, motionless, just watching her dad say goodbye to his date, or his girlfriend, or whoever she was. When he opened the door for her and escorted her out to a cab, Margot quickly moved toward her room and darted inside. She lay down in bed and pretended to be asleep, even though she knew he wouldn't check on her anyway.

ʔ

On Christmas Day, Margot got up and walked into the living room to find her dad there for the first time. There was a little squeeze in her chest as she remembered what she'd seen the night before, but she managed a tight smile. Trying to talk to him about it would be pointless and would no doubt just result in a fight, so Margot didn't bother.

"Well, well, well," said Margot, pulling up a stool at the breakfast bar, "look who decided to stay home with his errant spawn."

"Merry Christmas to you, too," said her dad drily. He poured cereal into a bowl with one hand and flipped through a paper with the other. Margot sat across from him, grabbed a bowl, and filled it to the brim with cereal before crushing a Pop-Tart on top of it. Her dad raised an eyebrow, no doubt at the amount of sugar she was about to consume, but he kept his mouth shut. Margot glanced into the living room, but from what she could see it all looked the same. No one had come by and put up a Christmas tree while she was sleeping, or hung a stocking.

"I got you something," said her dad, breaking her out of her reverie. Margot blinked, surprised.

"Oh, Dad, you didn't have to. I mean I didn't expect anything," said Margot, as her dad left the table. Despite herself, she smiled and felt the familiar flush creeping up her neck. She wasn't even embarrassed, but this whole redhead thing came with its own set of perks that she couldn't seem to control. *What could he possibly have gotten me?* It had been years since he'd gotten her a big gift—it was usually her mom who took care of that stuff.

"Alright, here we are," said her dad, coming back to the table. He set down a small card in a shiny little case. Margot raised her eyebrows, and reached for the card. Sliding it open, she saw it was a three hundred dollar Visa gift card. There was no note, and no wrapping paper. Not even a bow—just a card with the amount scrawled on it. Margot looked up at her dad, who was already reading the paper again. Her heart felt like it was sinking into her stomach.

"Are you kidding me?" said Margot.

Her dad glanced up at her dispassionately, turning the page.

"What's the matter?"

"What's the matter? Are you serious?"

"If it's not enough, Margot, I'll give you more. There's no need to make a scene."

"I don't need your money," said Margot. Against her will, hot tears sprung to her eyes and just made her angrier. "I mean, I do, obviously for tuition and stuff, but I have spending money of my own. I don't need your stupid gift card."

"Fine, Margot, fine," snapped her dad, his temper flaring as quickly as her own. "I don't know what you want me to do, here. I'm not sure what it was that I did wrong."

"This is the best you could do, really?"

"The best I could do at what?"

"At making this visit an actual holiday. I haven't seen you in four days, Dad. And now it's Christmas and you want to be able to slap some cash down on the table and expect me to fall on my face from joy?" *And you brought some woman here last night, and you didn't even tell me you were seeing someone.* Margot knew she wasn't being nice, but all her frustration from the trip was exploding at once.

"Every other girl I know enjoys receiving gift cards," said her dad stiffly. "It seemed like a pretty intuitive gift, rather than me getting you something you'd just return."

"I wouldn't have returned it!" Margot protested, laughing despite herself. "I would have been happy to get anything from you that showed you took more than thirty seconds to pick it out."

"You're being hysterical," her father said coldly. "You're acting just like your mother."

It was like he'd slapped her.

Margot looked at her dad, at the way his eyes were narrowed at her and his hands were clenched into angry fists. This was a man who was comfortable in a boardroom, in front of a judge, or in a room with two strangers going for each other's throats in divorce court, but was ill at ease with his own daughter. For the first time, Margot actually felt a little sorry for him. He didn't see that she was feeling neglected and angry because she'd barely seen him in the time she'd been here. All he saw was that he'd given her money and that she wasn't grateful for it. He wanted his quiet and peaceful condo back, without her presence here to mar it.

"I'm going to go," said Margot.

There was a brief silence.

"What are you talking about?"

"I want to fly back to school. Now, today."

Her dad stared at her with cold eyes.

"Margot, calm down. School hasn't even started up again yet."

"I don't care when it starts," said Margot. She was shaking now, her chest aching with anger. "I can't stay here another minute with you."

Margot was so hurt that her fists were clenched, and her vision was blurred.

"I think you're being a little dramatic."

"A little like my mother, you mean?" Margot shot back. "Maybe that's why you can barely look at me. I do look an awful lot like her."

"You know what? Go. You're my daughter, and if

you're going to act this way, I don't want you here, anyway."

"Fine," said Margot, her eyes filling with angry tears. "Merry Christmas, Dad," said Margot, and then she got up to get her things from the bedroom.

She was leaving.

Chapter Eleven

When Ophelia opened the door to the suite, Margot thought she'd never been more excited to see someone in her entire life.

"Fi!"

Ophelia turned and hugged Margot with one arm, dragging a massive piece of luggage with the other. The two nearly fell over as their legs tangled, and the stony-faced porters ignored them completely as they continued to bring in the rest of Ophelia's things.

"How was your break?" asked Ophelia, dropping

down onto the couch as her luggage was carried into her room.

Margot shrugged. "Well, you know."

"Mine sucked," sighed Ophelia. "You'd think by now I'd be used to having parents I hate, but it continues to be a surprise just how idiotic they can be."

Margot was surprised; she didn't think she'd ever heard Ophelia talk about her family before. She'd just figured there was some sort of moratorium on talking about families that were basically royalty or something.

"My dad wasn't very nice to me, either," Margot admitted. After the scene on Christmas Day, she'd used the dumb gift card he'd given her to buy herself a flight for that day out of San Francisco. He'd called a couple of times since then, she would give him credit for that, but Margot had no desire to talk to him. There was still no word from her mother.

"Well, you can be a part of my club, then," said Ophelia. She looked tired, Margot thought, with circles under her eyes and her dark hair pulled up into a messy ponytail. Margot knew she wasn't a lot to look at right now, either. She hadn't had much of an appetite in days, no matter what the chefs in the dining hall put down in front of her.

"So, how long have you been back?"

"A week or so," said Margot.

"What have you been doing by yourself this whole time?"

"Oh, you know. Homework and stuff like that."

That wasn't a total lie. The week that Margot had spent in basic isolation at Beverly Hills Prep had given her a lot of time to finish up on homework she was behind on, and also to consider other aspects of her life here. Something had snapped in Margot over the break; something had changed. Playing by the rules seemed less and less appealing.

Instead of fighting what made her stand out in this school, she should be capitalizing on it. It was the only way that she was going to be noticed by anyone. Being invisible was getting old. She couldn't change the amount of money her family had, or the social status that she'd been born into. But she could make a name for herself in other ways. When Margot arrived back at Beverly Hills Prep to a largely empty campus, she decided to go about making that happen.

The school that Margot had lived at for over two years had more secrets than she'd imagined; she'd spent days exploring every nook and cranny of the libraries, wandering in the chapel, and walking the grounds. It seemed like there were entire buildings and wings that had popped up out of nowhere, and now that Margot had had the time to look through it all, it was like an entirely new part of campus had opened up to her.

She'd discovered hallways that led right back into each other to form a giant continuous circle, and other shortcuts that detoured right to an exit or to a hidden corridor. It had taken days to map it all out in her mind, but with almost no one else around there was no better time to do it. Today all the resident students had started pouring in again, and Margot's solitude vanished.

"Well, I'm exhausted," said Ophelia. "So I'm going to bed. I'll see you for classes in the morning. I can't believe it's already the second semester."

"Me either," admitted Margot. "Good night. Let's make it to breakfast tomorrow; the chef said she's making French toast with orange butter and raspberry filling."

"Perfect. I'll be there."

Ophelia's door shut behind her, and Margot went into her bedroom. Looking around at the mess, Margot figured she could've taken some of her free time to clean, but it was a little late for that. She'd have to stick with the tried-and-true strategy of stuffing everything into her closet for inspections. Pulling out her phone, Margot typed out a quick text:

Can we meet tonight? I have info for you.

She sent it to Grace.

Margot took one of her new shortcuts to meet Grace. She wanted to avoid the crowds of girls lining the hallways. The corridors were full of the noise of roommates greeting each other and crammed with porters bringing luggage in. Every single girl seemed to have about four more suitcases than they needed; was Margot seriously the only girl in this place who knew how to pack an appropriate amount for a trip? Margot took a left turn where she normally would've gone right, and the chaos faded away behind her.

This corridor was dimly lit, spooky even, and there was a hidden door on the right side somewhere along here. Margot felt with her fingertips behind an enormous hanging tapestry of some king or another who was probably distantly related to Ophelia, and finally she grasped a doorknob that creaked open at her touch. The door led to another, narrower hallway, almost like a servant's passage, and then to another door that took her directly outside to the west side of the dormitory. This is where she normally met Grace, out of sight of the main walkway.

Grace was waiting with her back against the building.

"So, what's up?" said Grace. "Did you sell those wallets already?"

"Not yet," said Margot casually. "But I have a proposition for this whole thing."

"What's up?"

Margot was feeling reckless, and even though she knew this was a bad idea, she didn't seem to care anymore.

"There are a million hidden places in this school," said Margot. "I'm talking secret passages, rooms, everything. I could be distributing purses and getting the money back to you way faster and more efficiently, without us having to meet in person all the time."

"I don't really think my family is interested in your business advice," said Grace. "What's bringing this about, anyway? The last time we talked you were begging to get out of this."

Margot thought about the sound of the woman's

laughter that she'd heard that night at her dad's apartment. There was a twinge of worry for Ophelia—she wouldn't like this, and Margot didn't want to lose her as a friend. But Ophelia just didn't understand what it was like to exist on the fringes of Beverly Hills Prep; Margot might have been admitted to the school, and she might take classes here and eat and sleep here, but she still lived on the very edge of what this world had to offer. No grade point average or even amount of money could make up for the fact that she hadn't been born into the sort of family that belonged here.

So, she might as well take advantage of the situation she was currently in instead of wishing that she'd be accepted as something she wasn't. She didn't want to try anymore.

"I changed my mind," said Margot breezily. "This place is too boring without this little gig, anyway."

"That's good to hear," said Grace.

"But seriously, you should consider what I'm saying. We could be making automatic drops—leaving orders for customers in hidden spots and having them leave money in return instead of doing everything by hand."

"Then there's no way to make sure people will pay. How do you know they'll leave the money there and not just take the purse and leave?"

"Because they have money," said Margot. "They don't care about paying what you ask. These purses are already being sold for cheaper than they are in a store. And if they tried not paying, everyone would hear about it, and it would be embarrassing. They have the cash. They'll pay."

Grace studied her carefully. "I'll see what Kara says," she answered. "Speaking of which, she'll be at a little get-together we're having this weekend in one of the suites in the Oceanside dorm."

"Oh, really?" said Margot.

"Yeah," said Grace, casually shifting her weight onto her hip. "It'll be casual. We'll put a movie on and just hang out."

"Oh, cool."

"Friday night," said Grace. "I'll see you there. We can do your drop then. And I'll pass along your little idea to Kara."

"The demand is there," said Margot. "I run out of merchandise most of the time and still have girls asking for stuff."

"True. Alright, well I'll see you Friday then."

Chapter Twelve

Margot aced her quizzes the week after Christmas break, largely because she'd actually taken the time to study. For the first time all year, she was caught up in every class, and even ahead in a few. But this was Beverly Hills Prep, and it was the most prestigious prep school on the West Coast for a reason; by the time Friday rolled around, Margot had three projects and a paper that she needed to start working on to be turned in over the coming weeks. She rubbed her face with a hand as she left her last class on Friday afternoon; even being prepared, this week had been difficult.

"Ms. McKittrick! Margot!"

Oh no.

She had an after-school session today with her Pre-Calculus teacher that she'd completely forgotten about. Briefly, Margot considered pretending like she hadn't heard and continuing on her way, but after the talk with Headmistress Chambers, that didn't seem like a good idea.

"I'm coming, Mrs. Gable," sighed Margot, and she turned around to walk back into the classroom.

ᚲ

By the time Margot made it back to her and Ophelia's suite, it was nearly time to start getting ready for the party. She dropped her book bag on the floor with a sigh, and unbuttoned the top buttons on her shirt. The vest felt like it was choking her to death today. Her stomach rumbled, but Margot ignored it. Food had been making her a little sick lately, no matter what she ate. The door opened and Ophelia walked in, looking just as tired as Margot.

"Rough day?" Margot asked.

"What makes you say that?"

"You just look a little tired."

"I am," Ophelia admitted, sitting down on the couch.

"What are your plans for the night?" asked Margot.

"I don't really have any. Just working on a few paintings, maybe, for this showcase thing I'm in."

"Well, I'm going to a party if you want to go."

Ophelia hesitated, chewing her lip.

"You don't have to come or anything if you don't want to," Margot assured her. "It's just on campus, in one of the girls' rooms. I'm sorry, I don't even know if you wanted to do anything tonight—I just wanted to invite you."

"I probably won't stay long," said Ophelia, "but I could come for a little while."

"Really? Okay, perfect. I'm going to start getting ready and we can go over there a little later."

"What are you wearing?"

"I don't know. Jeans?"

"Oh, honey," said Ophelia. "Let me help you."

By the time evening rolled around, Margot was dressed in one of Ophelia's fancy party dresses and sparkly flats. Britney Spears pumped in the background, one of Ophelia's guilty pleasures, Margot had recently learned.

"Are you sure I don't look weird?" Margot said. "I feel like I look too fancy."

"You don't. It looks great on you," said Ophelia. "And you're taller than I am, so the length actually works better for you than it does me." The dress was navy blue, with long sleeves, and the color helped dim the brightness of Margot's red hair. Margot put the finishing touches on her makeup and fixed a curl with another spritz of hairspray, and then she was ready. Ophelia was wearing black leggings and a tunic that somehow managed to drape over one shoulder and make her look like a living painting; her hair was sleek and long in comparison to Margot's waves of curls.

"Are you ready to go?" Ophelia asked.

"Yeah, just give me one more second."

As Ophelia swiped on coral lip gloss that accentuated her pale skin, Margot felt a flash of apprehension. If Kara really did show up tonight, that was going to be the first time Margot had seen her since she graduated. It seemed like so much had happened since Margot had last seen her. Margot also made sure to grab the wad of bills from this week's sales and stuff them into her own bag. She needed to give it to Grace tonight at the party.

"Okay," said Margot, taking one last look in the mirror. "I'm ready."

ℝ

The party was in full swing by the time Margot and Ophelia knocked; Margot suspected that Nicole, whose room it was, had a few friends who were prefects and had promised not to give her a noise violation. The movie inside was blaring, and Margot could hear girls laughing all the way out in the hallway.

"Hi, Margot," said Nicole. Nicole was a senior who knew Margot by association. "Come in. And you brought a friend, I see."

"You know Ophelia Koroleva, Nicole, don't you?" said Margot over the noise. "She's my roommate."

"I think I know her parents at least," said Nicole. "Nice to have you here, Ophelia."

Ophelia smiled tightly but didn't respond; Margot got the feeling she didn't like her parents being mentioned. Well, Margot wasn't in any position to judge anyone else's relationship with their family.

"Help yourselves to some punch, or soda," said Nicole, and then she was gone, sashaying over to the other side of the room to a group of girls. There were a few boys in here, too, Margot noticed. They were allowed in during limited hours with passes. Margot and Ophelia both grabbed a soda from the side table, and as Margot sipped hers, she counted what must have been at least thirty people all squeezed into the common room.

"I'll be right back. I need to find the bathroom," said Ophelia to Margot. Margot nodded, sipping her soda as Ophelia walked away, trying to see if she could see anyone she knew. It was awkward standing here all by herself.

"Hi, stranger," said a voice over her shoulder, and Margot turned to see Kara with Grace just behind her. It did give her a jolt, seeing Kara again, but she smiled and opened her arms for a hug.

"Hello, yourself," said Margot. She saw Grace glaring at Ophelia, still making her way out of the room. Ophelia glanced back and noticed, but just smiled sweetly from across the room. Grace had hated Ophelia nearly on sight since the beginning of the year and Margot had no idea why. Whatever it was,

Ophelia could handle herself. Grace was just a guard dog—all bark and no bite.

"Nice party," said Kara casually.

"Yeah, absolutely," said Margot.

"It's been a long time," said Kara. "How is everything?"

"Everything is good," said Margot. She didn't really want to get into the details of her parents' divorce with Kara. After everything that had happened with the two of them, Margot respected her, but that didn't mean she trusted her. "What about you?"

"Oh, going just fine," said Kara. "Just making sure the family business is running smoothly."

"Speaking of which, I have a drop for you," said Margot, glancing at Grace. She pulled out the plastic bag of cash and handed it to Grace.

"Grace said you had some ideas for expanding within the school," said Kara. Margot couldn't quite tell from her tone what her thoughts were on the subject, so she stayed quiet and nodded.

"Yeah, I have some ideas," Margot said. "I just think there are a lot of opportunities present to use the campus itself, instead of having Grace and me handle every single thing personally. Like, there are all these passages and corridors that no one really knows about. There are nooks under urns and little hideaways behind paintings that we could use."

And you wouldn't need me as much, Margot found herself thinking. *What if the system I came up with to make a name for myself actually becomes my ticket out of this thing?* Margot hadn't even thought of that. *I want to do this,* she reminded herself. *I don't want to get out of it anymo*re. But was that the truth?

"So, you don't think the way we do things now is good enough?" said Kara, so smoothly that at first Margot didn't notice the bite in her tone.

"No, of course I do. I mean, the system in place now works fine."

"But you think you could make some improvements."

"Maybe," said Margot, hesitant now. Grace was

standing with her arms folded, looking over at the two of them.

"Look, Marg," said Kara, "I appreciate the view toward growth, I really do. I like your commitment toward what we're doing. But you aren't being paid to have these kinds of thoughts. We're paying you to sell the purses, and that's it."

Margot felt her face flaming.

"Uh, okay," she said. "I didn't mean anything by it. I just thought it might make sense."

"That's not your concern," said Kara smoothly.

Margot squared her shoulders, trying to look bolder than she felt.

"Fine, okay," said Margot, irritated now. "There's no need to act like I'm stupid."

"You're not," sighed Kara. "You just need to focus on what we're asking you to do, and not on anything else."

"I asked to get out of this whole thing, and Grace said I couldn't."

"What's your point?"

"I'm just saying—I said I wanted out of this whole thing, and you guys wouldn't listen to me," Margot protested.

"But then you changed your mind, didn't you?" Kara accused her.

Margot wasn't sure how to answer. She had changed her mind, but at a time when she was really upset, and not thinking clearly.

"Well, yeah, I guess—"

"Then there's no problem. Keep doing what you're doing; you're good at it. Now let's go mingle with everyone else. It's a party, after all."

Margot opened her mouth to retort, but they were already turning away. As Kara walked away, Margot struggled to remember why she'd ever felt like this girl was one of her friends. Had she made the right choice by changing her mind, and telling Grace she would keep selling purses? Margot wasn't sure anymore.

Chapter Thirteen

Margot woke up to a loud knocking on her door, and she opened it to Ophelia.

"We have room inspection in fifteen minutes," said Ophelia. "I figured you'd need the time to get your room ready."

"Thanks for the warning," said Margot, yawning. "Where'd you go last night?"

By the time she'd finished talking to Kara and Grace, she'd looked for Ophelia and hadn't seen her. Margot had stayed for a while and watched the movie, but it was pretty boring.

"Oh, I just came back here and went to sleep," said Ophelia. "I didn't really feel like staying."

"Yeah, it was pretty boring," said Margot.

Ophelia hesitated.

"I saw you talking to Grace," said Ophelia. "And I saw you hand her something."

"Yeah, I owed her a few bucks. She bought me lunch a couple days ago," Margot lied.

"Okay," said Ophelia. "But I saw you guys talking. I don't know. It didn't look like you and that other girl were just chatting. And they did not look like nice people."

"They aren't exactly my friends," said Margot. "We were just talking for a couple minutes."

"Margot, I've talked to you about this. Those girls are bad news—I would know, I used to get into trouble a lot, too. I don't care that Grace is rude to me. That's not the issue. She's not a good person."

"It's not as big a deal as you're making it out to be," Margot protested. "And I'm not really in the mood to fight with you about it." With a sick feeling, she realized that she reminded herself of her father in this moment. She sounded like him.

"Fine. I wasn't trying to fight with you," said Ophelia. "I was just trying to talk to you."

Ophelia toyed with her shirt hem, leaning in Margot's bedroom doorway.

"Look, Marg," she said, "I've talked to you about this a few times. And you said you were going to distance yourself from Grace and whatever she's involved in, and it seems like the opposite is happening."

"Ophelia, come on," said Margot. "I think you're just dramatizing things."

"I don't think I am," said Ophelia, her eyes honest and sad. "I think my instincts are right, and they're saying that you're more involved with Grace and that other girl than you want to admit, and involved in something bad. But Margot, I can't stay here with you in that kind of situation. I'm going to have to switch rooms."

"Fi, you don't mean that." *You're my only real friend here.* "Do you?"

"I do, Margot, and I'm sorry."

"You're not seriously going to move out," said Margot, starting to panic. "You aren't involved in anything, though. You aren't doing anything wrong," said Margot desperately, but she knew Ophelia was right. She'd made the decision not to stop after Christmas break, and Ophelia was going to have to move out because of it.

Ophelia shook her head silently.

"I'm sorry, Margot, I really am, but this is how I feel," said Ophelia. "I won't say anything to anyone. But if I can find a way to move out of here with minimum questioning, I will. I don't think me staying here is a good idea anymore."

Ophelia's eyes were swimming with tears, but her voice was firm. She shut Margot's door gently, and Margot collapsed back onto her bed. She felt too miserable to do anything but lay there, letting Ophelia's words rattle around in her aching head like echoes of a terrible song she couldn't forget. Eventually, she fell into a dreamless sleep.

When Margot woke up again, the sky outside her window was completely dark. She sat up slowly, her head still aching. Her phone said it was after eight at night—she must have literally slept through the entire day. Rubbing her face, Margot eased herself out of bed and shuffled to the bathroom. After a hot shower, she felt a little more human, but her bones felt achy, like she was a hundred years old. It all seemed like it had been a bad dream—the party, the conversation with Ophelia, everything. It was like it had all happened to someone else.

Margot pulled on sweatpants and a shirt and knotted her hair in a bun. Grabbing her laptop, she walked unthinkingly into the common room. All she wanted to do was watch a movie with her headphones in and then go back to sleep, but as she headed for the couch, she stopped short. Ophelia was already sitting there, staring intently at a canvas that she was covering with charcoal. She glanced up to see Margot there, and for a moment all they did was stare at each other. Margot didn't know what to do—*was she just supposed to stop acting like Fi was her friend?*

"Look, does it really have to be this way?" said Margot. "You just aren't going to talk to me for the rest of the year? There has to be a better option than this."

"You could stop being involved with Grace and her little posse," said Ophelia.

Margot didn't know what to say. She'd gone back and forth on how she felt about selling these purses to girls so many times, that she wasn't even sure how she felt about it anymore. At this point, the thought of not doing it anymore was a little hard to imagine.

"That's what I thought," said Ophelia, and she went into her bedroom, locking the door behind her. Margot closed her eyes as a rush of hot tears spilled down her cheeks. She wished she had something, anything, to keep from feeling the ache in her chest at the look on Ophelia's face.

Chapter Fourteen

Margot tapped her pen on her paper, staring aimlessly at the clock on the wall and praying that it would suddenly start ticking faster. One knee was bouncing and the other foot was tapping restlessly. Her quiz lay half filled out in front of her, but Margot couldn't bring herself to complete the rest. A million thoughts flooded her mind at once, and she tried to grab onto them as they passed, but they seemed to fly by before she could. She felt like she was going to launch right out of her own skin at any moment. Idly, she picked at a scab on her thumb.

"Please hand up your tests," said the teacher just

as the bell rang. "That means you back there. Thank you."

Margot shoved hers into the hand of the girl in front of her, and then practically sprinted out of the room. If she had to sit still another minute she was going to lose her mind. She was supposed to drop a Prada wallet off for someone, and she was late.

In the few weeks that had passed since the party, Margot found herself selling even more merchandise than usual. It was like the fight with Ophelia had pushed her over a line or something. Everything with her parents was still a mess, and it all just seemed too difficult to handle, so Margot was focusing her energy elsewhere—regardless of the consequences. And, she had a plan that was going to make Kara and Grace realize that her suggestion was a good one, and that she was someone to be taken seriously, not just brushed off.

Another thirty seconds of walking, and Margot saw what she was looking for: a sign for a bathroom. She ducked into the third-corridor restroom, which was only one stall. Inside, Jenna was waiting, her hands on her hips.

"You're late," she hissed. "I need the wallet for this weekend. I told all my friends that my boyfriend bought it for me, and they're going to ask to see it this weekend."

"Chill, Jenna. I have it here."

Margot handed over the red wallet, and Jenna gave her the money, which Margot flipped through.

"You know it's all there," Jenna said.

"We raised the prices. You owe me another twenty."

"Since when?"

"Since now."

Jenna raised an eyebrow at her, and Margot stared right back, shrugging her shoulders. It was all part of the new, secret plan.

"Look, I don't make the rules, okay?"

"Fine," sighed Jenna. She slapped another twenty into Margot's hand and left the bathroom. Margot waited a minute in the quiet room, and then checked

her watch. It was time to drop off the money with
Grace.

ſ̲

"You're late," snapped Grace as Margot met her in
the parking lot.

"I know, sorry," said Margot. "Jenna was late for
the drop-off."

Grace held out a hand, and Margot gave her the
cash. Grace flipped though the bills critically, frown-
ing at Margot. She didn't seem to realize that all the
money wasn't there—it was all part of Margot's long-
term strategy, so it was important that Grace didn't
notice in this moment and ruin everything.

"Okay. Looks fine. I'll see you later."

Grace wasn't very good at math; it looked like it
would be a while before anyone picked up on what
was happening. And by then, they'd all realize what
a great idea it was. Margot would show them. She
would show everyone.

Over the next couple of weeks, Margot refined her secret strategy even further. She was selling purses on her own, using the walls of Beverly Hills Prep itself to help her. It was the idea she'd pitched to Grace and Kara that they'd turned down. Margot wasn't sure what would happen if they caught on to what was happening before she was ready to tell them, but it wouldn't be pleasant. That fact motivated her to keep going, to have something to show for the all the risk. Grace didn't even seem to notice that Margot's order list was growing by the day.

Margot used the space behind the tapestry, the bottom of the eighteenth-century urn, and the hidden door in the third right corridor to hide merchandise, among other places. She left the requests from customers in those places, letting them all know over text where they could find their order. A few of them still received personal transactions, just in case Grace was paying attention.

But the rest, she let Beverly Hills Prep do for her. All she had to do was get the orders to the hiding places once a week or so, and then come back the next day for the cash. It was less time-consuming than trying to meet different girls all over campus, and with time, Margot was confident that Grace and Kara would see that.

It did take her a while to get all the purses and wallets into all the hiding places, but she had a map in her head of all the different places. Writing them all down was too risky—if anyone got hold of it, the whole covert operation would be ruined. So, it all stayed in her head, organized into little pictures in her brain. Before bed, Margot would flip through each one, making sure none were forgotten.

She was also raising prices, and she hadn't told Grace that either. Margot had definitely been right about one thing: their customer base had enough money to not care about the price jump. Even if

Grace and Kara didn't end up going for this idea, prices should still be raised, if Margot had anything to say about it. Most of the girls didn't even notice that Margot was asking for more, or if they did notice, they didn't care. Margot calculated the extra and kept it in hiding places within the school, so that she could show Kara and Grace the impressive total. Some of her clients had asked to pay her electronically, but Kara had a strict cash-only rule. She said it was just more convenient, and Margot didn't care much either way.

The weekdays started to fall into a pattern; Margot went to bed late, woke up and had coffee, and went to her morning classes. Then she'd suffer through her afternoon classes before spending the rest of her time either attempting to study or dealing with transactions. Studying was hard, though. For some reason, Margot was having a lot of trouble concentrating. It was like every time she sat down and tried to focus, all she could think about were all the things going wrong in her life. Her issues with her dad and her sadness about her mom all combined to make it harder and harder to get any schoolwork done. Margot tried to buckle down and fight it, but it wasn't easy.

One afternoon, Margot entered her and Ophelia's suite after her classes to find a scrawled note on the coffee table. Ophelia hadn't spoken to her since the morning after the party; Margot barely saw her. She spent all her time in her room or in the library. Picking up the note, Margot read the swirled handwriting as a bitter taste came into her mouth.

They're letting me move out. By the time you read this, my stuff will be gone. Good luck, Marg.

Love, Fi

Then there was a little drawing of a rose, delicate and tiny, and that was it. Ophelia had used to doodle them on all of Margot's notebooks, a petal at a time. Margot walked into Ophelia's room and her throat tightened as she stared into the empty space. There was nothing she could do now, though. Ophelia was gone. It was better this way, anyway. Now she didn't have to worry about getting her into trouble anymore. Everybody won in this situation, right? They both had what they wanted.

As Margot stepped out of Ophelia's room, brushing at suddenly watery eyes, she realized her phone was going off. She picked it up, expecting it to be one of her girls calling with an order, but her dad's number lit up instead. Margot groaned; this was not something she wanted to deal with right now. Or ever, for that matter. But she hadn't talked to him since Christmas break. Guilt had her answering the call, with a sigh.

"Hi, Dad."

"Hi, Margot."

There was an awkward silence.

"How are you?"

"I'm fine, Dad," said Margot, realizing how untrue that was. "How are you?"

"I'm fine, too."

He hesitated for a moment. Margot waited impatiently, tapping her foot.

"I wanted to apologize for Christmas break," he said. "I didn't intend for things to end the way they did."

"Dad, it's fine," said Margot. It wasn't, not really, but she didn't want to talk about it. It would just make things worse.

"We don't have to talk about it if you don't want to, but I wanted to tell you I'm sorry I wasn't home more. That was wrong of me."

"It's okay, Dad," said Margot quietly. She couldn't bring herself to ask about the woman. She wanted her dad to be happy—she really did. But she wasn't ready to ask about his dating life, yet. It was too weird. Besides, if he'd wanted her to know about it, he would've introduced the woman to Margot. And he hadn't.

"Have you heard from your mom?"

Despite herself, Margot's eyes filled with tears. "No. I haven't."

Her throat clenched, and suddenly it was hard to swallow.

"Oh, kiddo, I'm sorry," said her dad, and a tear rolled down Margot's cheek. "Your mom and I have our differences, but in all fairness, she's having a hard time right now. Just give her a little time and she'll come around."

Margot didn't know how to answer that. It wasn't that she didn't believe what her dad was saying, but her mom wasn't the only one who was having a hard time.

"Okay," said Margot. She appreciated the reassurance, but the fact that she still hadn't spoken to her mom was a hard subject right now, and not one Margot felt like discussing.

There was another pause. Margot studied her fingernails and waited for him to say something else, but there was nothing but silence.

"Look, I've got a lot of homework. I'll talk to you later, Dad, okay?"

She hung up before he could answer. She did have

homework to do. There was no point in thinking about all this stuff with her parents, anyway. Margot swung her backpack over her shoulder; she was going to go straight to the library and try to study for Calculus after dinner.

Chapter Fifteen

Margot snagged a tray in the dining hall and got in line; they were serving lamb-stuffed pears with cilantro and pomegranate tonight, along with buttercream and raspberry cake with a dark chocolate ganache for dessert. It smelled okay, but Margot still didn't have much of an appetite. But she couldn't exactly recall the last time she ate, so she needed to force something down her throat or she'd probably pass out in the middle of class or something else equally as embarrassing. Her stomach had been twisting with nerves lately, even at times when she didn't have anything to be anxious about, and it made eating difficult.

Grabbing a silver tray, Margot accepted a serving of the lamb-stuffed pears, rice pilaf with toasted orzo pasta, and a piece of the decadent-looking cake. Then she snagged a soda and went to sit down at the end of one of the long tables. It was painfully clear to Margot that now that Ophelia was gone, she had no real friends. Somehow, all that she'd done to involve herself with the girls that she thought were cool hadn't even worked. She was still on the outside looking in.

The third-years eating down the table from her were gossiping about some girl, and Margot suddenly couldn't stand another minute of it. She grabbed her headphones and plugged them into her ears, picking at her food and sipping on soda until she got up and left, most of her food still on her plate.

Margot woke up the next morning with a start, sitting straight up in bed. Her heart was pounding as though she'd just run a marathon, and for a second, she had no idea what day it was or what time it was. *When did I fall asleep?* The last thing she remembered clearly was sitting in bed and trying to study late into the night; she must have fallen asleep without realizing it. Grabbing her phone, Margot groaned as she saw the time. She was already ten minutes late to her first class, and she knew they were having a quiz today. Leaping out of bed, Margot grabbed a pleated skirt and a shirt and put them on as fast as she could, wishing she could go back to sleep instead. Yawning hugely, Margot corralled her hair into a ponytail and grabbed her book bag. In her bathroom mirror, her dark brown eyes were underscored with dark circles, and her cheeks looked hollow. Her hair was a wild mane, even tamed back with a hair tie. This would have to do—there wasn't time to worry about the fact that she looked like a zombie right now. Margot left the suite, slamming the door behind her.

"That wasn't so bad," she heard some girl say as they exited the classroom. "I think I over-studied, actually."

Margot rubbed her temples. She knew she'd missed at least half of those questions. Last night she'd studied for a long time, but nothing was sticking in her mind. It all slid away as soon as she read it, like spilled milk. Margot opened her phone to a text—someone wanted a pink Gucci purse, for tomorrow night. She texted them back that she could do that, and when she looked up again, she almost ran straight into Grace.

"What do you think you're doing?" Grace hissed through her teeth. She glanced at the crowd of girls flooding past them in the hallway and lowered her voice. "I need to talk to you."

"What is your problem?" said Margot. Grace pulled her into a deserted classroom and slammed the door behind them, and for a moment Margot felt panicked.

"I want to know what's been going on," said Grace. "I know you're messing with me somehow."

"What are you talking about? How have I been messing with you? I just met you for a cash drop like two days ago, and you gave me a bunch of my orders."

"I just saw Pearl showing everyone her Fendi clutch outside a classroom," said Grace. "You told me you were giving that to her in two days, so she shouldn't even have it yet. And you were nowhere near there when she had it. It looked like she had just picked it up from someone else, or something, or from an empty classroom. I don't know, but it looked weird to me."

Margot thought fast, her heart pounding. She'd dropped off that purse for Pearl in the urn in the left-hand corridor of the building that Grace was talking about. Pearl must have picked it up, and Grace had seen her.

"She asked for it a couple days early," said Margot. "She wanted to change the drop time, so I met her earlier than planned. That's it. There's nothing else going on. I swear."

"Are you sure? You didn't leave it for her somewhere? You know how Kara feels about that; every transaction needs to be personal. It needs to come directly from one of us, or else it opens up the floor for stealing and sloppiness."

Margot solemnly placed a hand over her heart. "I swear, I'm not leaving orders for girls to pick up. I know the rules. Sorry I didn't let you know ahead of time that Pearl wanted her order early; I didn't think it was a big deal."

Grace sighed, looking left and right before she turned back to Margot with a serious expression.

"It's just that things are a little, well, touchy right now. The faculty are starting to get wise. Apparently, the school has heard from a few parents who have noticed their daughters carrying purses they didn't buy for them, and it's making everyone suspicious."

Margot remembered the girls from last year talking about the same issue. The faculty was probably aware again that purses were circulating within the school somehow.

"Okay. So, what does that mean?"

"It means we all need to be very cautious. The faculty are on high alert for anything that looks suspicious, so for the time being, if you're giving a girl her order, make sure to do it somewhere very private. If you get caught, or if any of us get caught, we're all in big trouble."

Margot thought Grace was overreacting just a little—what they were doing was basically like eBay, wasn't it? People re-sold their own stuff all the time. It didn't seem like such a big thing, but Grace was obviously concerned, so Margot nodded solemnly. If Pearl hadn't made such a scene with her new bag, Margot wouldn't be dealing with this at all. The girl had almost messed up Margot's whole plan.

"I understand," said Margot. "No problem."

"Okay, good. We should go—I'll see you later."

Grace turned and left the classroom, and as soon as the door shut behind her Margot collapsed into a chair. She'd warned all her girls not to be obvious about picking up orders, or showing them off too much, but clearly, they weren't listening. That interrogation had almost given her a heart attack, and now Margot's hand was forced. She was going to have to reveal to Kara and Grace what she'd been doing earlier than she planned. Tonight, she could count how much extra she'd made and call Kara. Surely, when Kara saw that Margot's way of doing things made more sense, she'd be happy. How could she not be? Margot had singlehandedly upped the price of product while also making it easier to give out more merchandise at once.

Straightening her vest, Margot took a deep breath and left the classroom, checking to make sure no one was watching her go. She only had a couple of minutes before her next class. As Margot walked down the hallway, her phone lit up in her pocket. Margot's heart nearly stopped again. It was her mom.

Chapter Sixteen

Margot darted into a corridor in the Mathematics building, hiding herself behind a pair of velvet curtains. Taking a deep breath, she answered her phone.

"Mom?"

"Hi, Margot."

Margot clutched her phone with one hand, twisting her hair nervously with the other.

"Hi," she whispered, her eyes filling with tears despite herself. "Mom, how are you? It's so good to hear from you."

"It's great to hear your voice, honey," said

Margot's mom. "Listen—I'm sorry I haven't been in touch."

"It's okay," said Margot, even though she wasn't sure that it was. "But why? What's been going on with you?"

There was a long pause, and Margot bit her lip.

"Margot, the last year has been really hard on all of us," said her mother. "I know that your dad and I haven't always made it easy on you."

"Yeah, it's been rough. I know that."

"But honey, I finally hit my breaking point. That's when I left. I had to go so I could focus on myself and get myself together before I could move on with my life."

"I understand that," said Margot, "but why did you have to leave me behind? I get why you wouldn't want to talk to dad, but what about me? Why did you shut me out too?"

"That was the recommendation from my therapist, sweetie—that I temporarily focus solely on myself. I'm sorry if I hurt you, but it was something

I needed to do. And I always wanted to have joint custody with your dad, so when he suggested it, I thought you'd be happy that we weren't trying to make you choose."

"I was just confused as to why you left, and then wouldn't talk to me," said Margot. She could feel her temper rising; maybe her mom had done what she thought was right, but Margot disagreed with her methods. "Mom, that wasn't okay. You just left me."

"Margot, I'm sorry about that, I really am. Things can be different now. I want you to come out and visit me this summer, and we can talk as often as you want. It's going to be okay."

"I want to believe you, Mom, but I'm afraid to," Margot admitted, wiping at her nose. "I trusted you, and you left me. I can't just go back to the way things were."

"Sweetie, try to understand. Things with your father and I were a mess. I took some distance so that I could be a better mother to you, I swear it."

"Logically, I understand," said Margot, "but it still hurts. I'm still really, really mad at you."

"And you have the right to be. Look, take some time and think about things. Call me when you're ready, and I promise you I'll be here. I'll never leave you again, okay? I promise, Margot. Things will be better now."

"I want to believe you," Margot whispered. "I'll call you soon."

"Okay. I'm here. I love you."

Margot hung up, her hands shaking. Blowing out a deep breath, she tried to dry her tear-stained face. Hearing her mom's voice again had unleashed a tornado of the emotions that Margot normally tried to keep buried. It was almost too much to deal with, to hear her mother apologizing and explaining. Margot hadn't realized how truly hurt she was until this moment, and now, she didn't know how to deal with any of this. Margot checked her watch, still trying to stop crying. She was going to be late for Calculus.

Attempting to force her emotions aside, Margot took another deep breath.

I can handle this. It's no big deal. I'm fine. I'm totally fine.

Margot headed off to class, patting her cheeks dry, and trying to believe herself.

Chapter Seventeen

Margot stared at the question on her Calculus worksheet. It said something about limits, but the rest kept swimming in front of her eyes. She blinked, trying to clear it, but the cloudiness stayed. The rest of the class seemed to be reading it just fine; the girl to Margot's right was scribbling away. Margot's lip trembled as her mom's words replayed in her head over and over again.

Stop it. You need to focus, she told herself.

"Hey, are you okay?"

The girl sitting next to Margot looked concerned,

and Margot realized she must not be hiding her emotions as well as she usually was.

"Yeah, I'm fine," said Margot, but her chest was tightening, and she couldn't seem to breathe normally all a sudden.

"Ms. McKittrick, is there an issue back there?" said Mrs. Gable, looking up from her desk.

"No, not at all," Margot answered. She turned back to her worksheet, struggling to focus, but her chest continued to tighten, and Margot could feel herself tearing up all over again. Her chest began to make a wheezing noise, and Margot rubbed it, trying to loosen the pressure.

"Ms. McKittrick," said Mrs. Gable, concerned. "Are you alright?"

The teacher got up from her desk and approached Margot, who was now actively crying, and wheezing for breath at the same time. Other girls were beginning to stare and whisper, but Margot couldn't seem to get herself to calm down.

"I'm okay," she tried to say, but all that came out was a choked sob.

"Margot, try and calm down. You're pale as a sheet. Here, let me get you a paper bag. I think you're having a panic attack."

The teacher brought Margot a paper bag and told her to breathe into it; Margot tried, embarrassment dimly registering, but she still couldn't calm down. All the stress she'd been trying to ignore or push away was coming out at once, and she couldn't control it anymore. She was crying openly now, her hands trembling, and finally Mrs. Gable stopped her.

"Okay, dear. We need to take you to the nurse, okay? Everyone, please continue to work on your worksheets. I'll be back momentarily."

Margot struggled to her feet, Mrs. Gable's hand under her elbow. It was still hard to breathe, and little spots were dotting her vision.

"I'm feeling very light-headed," said Margot as they walked out of the classroom.

Oh, please don't let me faint in class.

"Just hang on," said the teacher as they continued walking. "We'll get you to the nurse right now."

A door opened, and Margot realized they'd entered the administrative building. The nurse's office was down the hallway, past the door. Margot was vaguely aware of entering the room and the nurse jumping up to help her into a seat, but nothing seemed clear.

"I'm not sure what the problem is," said Mrs. Gable. "She was sitting in class, and then I noticed that she was upset. It looks like that turned into a full-blown panic attack."

"I'm inclined to agree with you," said Nurse Lori. "Margot, dear, go ahead and put your head between your legs. That's it—now try and breathe slowly. Here are some tissues."

"I need to get back to my classroom," said Mrs. Gable to the nurse. "Do you need anything else before I go?"

"No, it's alright. I can take it from here. Thanks for bringing her in."

"Margot, stay here with the nurse, okay? I'll make sure you're excused for as long as you need. Feel better, dear."

Then she was gone, and it was just the nurse and Margot together. As Margot sat with her head between her legs, trying to breathe, the nurse wrapped something around Margot's arm and it squeezed her, beeping at the same time.

"I'm just taking your blood pressure and your pulse, okay, Margot?"

Margot nodded as best she could from her awkward position. Her chest was beginning to feel less like she was being squeezed, and she sat up, taking her first full breath since the attack began.

"Honey, I think you just experienced a panic attack," said Nurse Lori. "Your pulse is starting to go down now, but your blood pressure is still high. Has this ever happened to you before?"

"No," said Margot. "Not really."

"Do you have any idea why you think this

happened? Is something going on with you that you'd like to talk about?"

Margot shook her head, but the tears filled her eyes all over again. She found herself haltingly telling Nurse Lori about the phone call with her mom, the divorce, and how hard things had been at school. She carefully left out saying anything about the purses, too afraid to share that secret with a school official.

"It seems like you're under a great deal of stress, Margot," said the nurse. "I'm surprised you haven't been seeing a therapist since the initiation of your parents' divorce. I would recommend regular counseling, and perhaps a prescription to help with your anxiety."

"Anxiety?"

"Margot, you look thin. Have you had trouble eating lately? Concentrating?"

Margot nodded. "How did you know that?"

"It's my job to know. I think your anxiety has been making it hard for you to function normally."

"I guess so," said Margot slowly. "Everything just

seemed to hit me at once. It was like everything was spinning out of control, and I couldn't stop it."

As she spoke, Margot reached into her still-open backpack, rummaging for tissues. Her sleeve got caught on a zipper, and as she yanked on it, her entire backpack spilled open. Clutches and wallets slid across the floor, and Margot frantically leaned over to grab them, stuffing them hurriedly into her backpack, but the nurse was faster.

"Margot, what is all this?" she asked, holding up a Dolce & Gabbana tote.

"It's nothing," said Margot. "Just gifts, from my dad. Anyway," she continued, trying to act casual, "I feel a lot better now."

There was a brief moment of total silence, and Margot could practically feel her panic playing across her face. She tried to keep making excuses about her purse collection, and her dad's penchant for buying them for her, but it didn't seem to be working. To her horror, the nurse did not look at all convinced by her protests. With a sickening feeling of dread,

Margot remembered that the faculty were on alert for things like this. Nurse Lori reached out and touched Margot's shoulder gently, and Margot stopped babbling.

"I think we need to call the headmistress, Margot," said the nurse quietly.

Chapter Eighteen

The seat in the headmistress's office was familiar, but that didn't comfort Margot as she sat on the cold wood, her legs wound round the feet. She clutched the sides of the chair so tightly that her fingers were turning numb. She had never been so scared in her entire life.

Margot tried to take a deep breath, tried to get her hammering heart rate to slow, but it was no use. She was on the verge of another panic attack. Her mind raced furiously, jumping from worry to worry.

Do I have any purses in my room?

No, I don't, thank goodness. Every last one was dis-tributed except the ones in my stupid backpack.

How could I be so careless?

Calm down, Margot told herself. *They don't know anything for sure. Maybe it will all be okay.*

Part of her wanted to just confess to all of it. Then there wouldn't be this terrible period of waiting for what seemed like hours to find out her fate. Next to her, the nurse sat holding her clipboard, and the headmistress was on her way in from a meeting.

What's going to happen? thought Margot, and she bit her lip to keep from crying.

The door finally swung open, and Headmistress Chambers swept in like a queen, her eyeglasses perched on her nose, her eyes piercing.

"I apologize for the slight delay," she said. "I was in a meeting."

"I'm sorry to disturb you, Headmistress," said the nurse, "but we have a bit of a strange situation here."

The headmistress took in the sight of Margot

quivering on the edge of the chair, her backpack at her feet.

"Mrs. Gable brought Margot in to see me, Headmistress. She was having what I believe to be a panic attack induced by stress and anxiety. Her blood pressure was high, and so was her pulse, though they've returned to close to normal levels now. Then, Margot's bag spilled open, and I saw all the purses. Margot said they were all gifts, but given the warning that the faculty was given regarding this kind of situation, I thought it was best to inform you."

The nurse's eyes weren't unkind as they surveyed Margot, but Margot still felt the hot rush of shame flood her body.

"Can I see your backpack, please, Margot?" said the headmistress.

Reluctantly, Margot handed it over, and the headmistress unzipped it and looked inside, shifting through Margot's belongings. Her eyebrows raised as she found the purses, and she looked at Margot.

"Margot, are all of these yours?"

"Yes, of course," Margot lied.

"Most still have the tags on them," said the headmistress. "Why do you have so many?"

"They were a gift," said Margot desperately, her lie coming undone. "I don't know why my dad got me so many—he just did."

"I suspect that if we traced all of these, they'd have come from a wide range of department stores in the area," said the headmistress. "Margot, I'm very disappointed."

"I didn't do anything," Margot protested, her face hot with shame.

"You're in possession of stolen property, Margot. And distribution of stolen property, I'd also assume."

Margot's mouth dropped open in shock. *Stolen property?*

You're so stupid, said a voice in her head. *Of course all this stuff is stolen. How'd you think they were getting it?*

I thought they were, like, buying it cheap somewhere

and then reselling it for more, thought Margot. *I didn't know it was all stolen!*

The headmistress turned to Margot, who couldn't help but shrink beneath her gaze.

Margot didn't know what to do. Did she tell the truth, and risk the consequences? Or did she lie, and hope they didn't find evidence that she wasn't being totally truthful? She didn't know which was better. Neither sounded ideal. The headmistress studied her carefully, and Margot felt as transparent as glass. This wasn't going to work.

"I don't know what you're talking about," said Margot. This was worse than she could've imagined. She wasn't familiar with laws regarding stolen property, but she did know that for her to have it in her own possession looked bad. Margot's eyes filled with tears for what seemed like the hundredth time that day. She was so ashamed. Never had she imagined that what she was doing was this bad, but now, she was definitely in a lot of trouble.

"I don't believe you, Margot," said the

headmistress quietly. "Why don't you tell me who gave these bags to you?"

Margot just shook her head. No way was she mentioning Grace's name. Grace was going to absolutely flip when she realized that Margot was in the headmistress's office at all. When she heard about the way Margot had acted in class, Margot didn't know what she would do. She felt ill just thinking about it. All her drops, all that cash was still waiting, hidden on campus. What was she going to do?

"Alright," said the headmistress smoothly. "Well, Margot, I'm going to call my contact on our private security team and see what he recommends. I'll also be calling your father to fill him in on the situation."

"Wait, what?" Margot rose out of her chair, panic choking her throat. "What are you talking about?"

"Margot, you're in possession of stolen property. Protocol demands that law enforcement get involved, and your father as well, since you're a minor."

Margot held her head in her hands; she'd never been so terrified.

I should've gotten out of this mess when I had the chance, she thought. Now, it was too late.

Chapter Nineteen

The headmistress agreed to call Margot's dad before the security team.

"I want a lawyer in the room when I'm speaking to them," said Margot, and she could've sworn she saw the headmistress smile, in a sort of exasperated manner.

"Very well. You are a minor—so your father can be present as both your lawyer and your parent, if you choose, although having a lawyer in the room isn't absolutely necessary. But our security team will be conducting a search of your dormitory without you present."

"Okay," said Margot. Thankfully, all of the merchandise she had in there was gone. There wasn't a trace purse anywhere in her room, she was sure of that.

"Can I use the restroom?" Margot asked the headmistress suddenly, as she thought about Grace.

"Yes, go ahead."

There was a restroom right next to the headmistress's office. Margot ducked inside and pulled her phone from her pocket. She'd gotten a few texts since she'd been in that office. Some were from girls (more like clients, really) who were asking if they should be worried about her getting called into the office; Margot ignored those and opened one from Grace.

What is going on?? Heard you got pulled out of class.

Margot felt a little flurry of fear over what she'd do if Margot ever did turn her and the rest of the operation in. No, Margot couldn't tell the headmistress anything. She was too scared. Typing as quickly as she could, she sent a text to Grace:

I'm in the headmistress's office, but everything is fine. I didn't say anything.

She sent it off and erased all her messages and every contact on her phone with shaking hands. If Grace had already heard about what happened, she had probably heard that Margot had been escorted out of class. The thought made Margot's stomach flip upside down. Hopefully Grace would be able to keep her head and not jump to any conclusions.

When Margot walked back into the headmistress's office, the headmistress was just hanging up her phone.

"The security team is on its way," said Headmistress Chambers smoothly, as casually as though she'd just announced that she liked Margot's hairstyle. Margot wondered how many times she had been in this exact situation, or at least a similar one. Probably too many times to count. "And I called your father."

"You already called him?"

"Yes."

"Well, fine then. What did he say?"

"A few choice words," said the headmistress, "but he's getting on a plane now. He should be here within two hours."

"Great," mumbled Margot.

"You can sit here until the security team finishes the search of your dorm room, and then they'll want to question you and search you and your book bag as well. They'll also want to take a look at your phone."

"What will they ask me?"

"They'll ask a number of things, Margot. It all depends on what they find during the search. That will be the start in determining what happens to you next."

Margot closed her eyes and wrapped her arms around herself; despite her efforts to stay calm, her body was literally trembling with nerves. She'd never wanted to end up like this. Tucking her legs underneath her, Margot settled in to wait, her heart thumping like a drum inside her ribcage.

An eternity was passing outside, Margot was sure of it, and she was still stuck in the headmistress's office. She'd given up trying to look calm and prim in her seat and was pacing instead, back and forth on the carpet like a caged animal. Headmistress Chambers watched but didn't comment.

Finally, after a thousand years had passed, there was a knock at the door.

"Enter," called the headmistress, and Margot's father strode inside.

"Dad," said Margot. He shot her a look that could've frozen fire.

"What is going on? I get a call saying you've got some stolen property or something and I need to come down here—what is happening, Margot?"

Margot twisted her hands in her skirt, feeling like she was about three years old. Instead of the familiar rush of anger she was used to, she was flooded with shame. It choked her voice and made her cheeks burn, and it was even worse than the fear she'd been enduring for the past four hours.

"I'm sorry, okay?" said Margot. "I'm sorry. I didn't mean for any of this to happen."

"Margot, tell us what's going on. Now," her dad snapped, rubbing a hand over his eyes. "You know I had to leave a very important meeting with a client to come here and deal with this?"

"Sorry I'm such a constant drain on your life," Margot said, her temper appearing with a welcome rush of anger. Anger was better than the panic.

"Where's the security team?" asked her dad.

"They're still going through Margot's dormitory."

Suddenly, Margot was grateful that Ophelia had moved out. She'd been right all along, about what would happen, hadn't she? At least she didn't have to be involved in Margot's mess.

Margot's dad shook his head; Margot had never seen him so angry, not even during the divorce.

"Can I see her backpack?" he asked the

headmistress, and to Margot's horror, she handed it over. Margot cringed as her dad pulled out designer bag after designer bag, shaking his head.

"According to Margot, those are gifts from you," said the headmistress quietly.

Margot's dad turned to glare at her.

"I didn't buy her any of these," he said. "Margot, you need to tell us the truth, now."

"I'm too scared," Margot whispered. "I'm afraid."

"Margot, nothing you say will leave this room," said the headmistress. "That's a promise. And if you are helpful to us, I can help make sure that this doesn't go on your permanent record, or worse."

Before Margot could say anything else, the security team arrived. The day was just getting worse and worse.

ᚱ

The next hour was nothing but total chaos. Three members of the private security team used by Beverly

Hills Prep were there to fill in the headmistress on Margot's room search.

"We didn't find anything else," the female guard said, and Margot breathed a quiet sigh of thankfulness. She'd been sure that there was nothing incriminating in there, but it was still a relief to hear. "It's a bit of a mess in there right now, so we're trying to get everything back in its place. Her roommate wasn't there, so no one was disturbed."

By now, Margot knew the whole school would be gossiping about her. The other girls who lived in that building were probably standing and watching the police search her entire suite. *Wow, this was embarrassing.*

"And this gentleman was kind enough to help with the bag search," said another guard wryly, kneeling to Margot's book bag.

"Nothing in there, Jordan. I checked it, too," said the female guard.

"The cell is totally wiped—nothing on there. We

can pull the phone records if necessary; it doesn't look like there's a need right now."

Another officer had Margot sitting down in the uncomfortable chair again as they all stared at her. The pressure of the headmistress, her father, and the security team was too much for Margot. She couldn't keep lying; it was too hard.

"Margot, are you ready to talk about what's going on?"

Margot nodded, and she started talking.

She refused to say anything about Grace, but Kara's name slipped out, and the headmistress recognized her as a past student. The rest, about how she'd just wanted to make friends and then had gotten caught in the spiral, just came spilling out, all the way up to her panic attack this morning.

"I swear, I never knew this stuff was all stolen," said Margot tearfully. "I honestly didn't. I just thought it was a stupid, fun sort of game. And then I tried to stop, and I couldn't. I'm sorry. I just didn't want to be lonely, anymore."

There was a long pause when she finished, and Margot thought she saw compassion in the headmistress's eyes.

"She's been under more stress than I realized, with the divorce," Margot's dad said quietly. "This panic attack—I don't think it was a coincidence. I think Margot has been independent for so long that I forgot she's just a kid."

Margot pressed her hands to her face, wiping away tears.

"I didn't mean for any of this to happen," she choked, and she knew that sounded dramatic, but she'd never been so terrified in her life. Her dad laid a hand on her shoulder, his expression solemn, but not unkind.

"Margot, why didn't you tell me you were struggling with anxiety?"

"I honestly didn't know it was a problem," Margot admitted. "I thought I was okay, and I just wasn't. I knew I was struggling, but I didn't realize it was as serious as it is. I thought I just needed to buckle down, and try harder to focus."

"Okay, all that aside, let's talk next steps regarding legal action," said the head of the security team.

"Let's see if we can't make some sort of agreement," said Margot's father firmly. Margot had never seen him handle a legal event before, but she had to admit it seemed like he knew what he was doing, even though he was a divorce lawyer and not a defense attorney.

"What she's told us is helpful," the guard admitted, and Margot lifted her head hopefully. "We will be sure to inform the proper authorities of the names that Margot released, and follow up on that. But she was still in possession of the property, and she admitted to distributing it as well."

"But she's by no means the head of the operation," protested her dad. "She's a kid who got caught up in something bad because of peer pressure, tried to escape from it, and couldn't. Along with that, she's dealing with untreated anxiety. I think she deserves leniency."

"I think it might be a good idea to book her and go from there," said another guard.

"Let's not get hasty," said Margot's father. "This is an underage schoolgirl, not a criminal. She has no record whatsoever. I think a suspension of some kind would be appropriate here."

"The suspension goes without saying," said one of the guards.

The headmistress folded her hands and remained silent.

"Then a suspension combined with continued therapy and counseling when she returns to school seems like a good compromise," said Margot's dad.

"No time in a juvenile correctional facility at all?" said an officer.

"For what? For being susceptible to peer pressure? Surely you don't book every teenager who makes a mistake."

The guard sighed. "I understand where you're

coming from. But these are expensive purses, and even if she didn't steal them herself, Margot should have known what she was doing was wrong."

"True, true. But Margot has no history of poor behavior until now, and I think that much of it has to do with the stressors in her life lately. The divorce, her loneliness, and anxiety all combined to lead to poor judgment. With a no-tolerance policy for another slipup, and continued scheduled counseling sessions with a psychologist, I think she'll get back on track and have no further issues."

There was more discussion, and Margot was left to sit on the chair, twisting her fingers together, to wait for the decision. The headmistress offered input to the discussion as they surrounded the table, and then the chief of security nodded tersely. They all turned as silence finally fell, looking at Margot like they'd forgotten she was there, which was ironic considering she was the cause of all of this. Margot shifted to the edge of her seat, brushing tears from her cheeks, to await her verdict.

Chapter Twenty

In the end, Margot agreed to a two-week suspension, bi-weekly counseling sessions with a therapist upon her return to school, and finishing out the rest of the year on academic probation. Her dad agreed to fund the rest of her year at Beverly Hills Prep since there were only a couple of months until summer, and the following year, her scholarship would be revisited. Margot's therapy appointments were mandatory, and they would work closely with Nurse Lori and a doctor to see if an anti-anxiety drug would be helpful for her.

Margot got the feeling that the security detail

thought she was a spoiled kid who deserved worse than she was getting, but the headmistress seemed to be sympathetic to what Margot had been dealing with in her personal life. Because she was a resident student at Beverly Hills Prep, the school would be entrusted with her curfew and enforcement of the rest of her requirements.

"Do you accept these terms?" the chief of security asked Margot. She swallowed, but nodded. The terms were strict, but honestly, she was relieved.

"I'll need these terms drawn up in writing," the guard was saying to the headmistress.

"Understood. We'll set the date and time. Thank you for your help today," said the headmistress. She ushered them out politely, and the door to her office clicked shut. The headmistress turned to look back at Margot and her father, and the room was suddenly quiet. Margot was shaking from adrenaline and exhaustion simultaneously; this had been one of the most harrowing mornings of her life.

"You can pack your things for your suspension,"

said the headmistress. "And here's your phone back, as well."

She handed Margot her cell phone back, and Margot shoved it into her pocket gratefully.

"We'll meet when you return and go over the schedule of your therapy appointments," said the headmistress.

"Do I have to leave now?"

"Yes. I'll escort you to your dormitory while you pack your things."

"Headmistress, I'm nervous about what I told you," said Margot. "I'm afraid the girls will know that I talked to you and that I got them in trouble." She was talking about Kara, whose name she'd mentioned as she admitted the truth.

"I don't want you worrying about that," said the headmistress. "We'll take care of it discreetly, and I promise you, we will never admit or share your involvement in that aspect. You can trust me."

Margot nodded, biting her lip. "Thank you."

"I'll start looking for another flight," sighed her father.

After walking back to her dormitory to pack, trailed by both the headmistress and her father, Margot felt separated from her body, like she was watching herself stuff clothes and shoes into a bag while they waited. Girls openly stared, whispering as she headed back toward the Great Hall with her luggage, and Margot couldn't blame them. She would be the talk of campus for weeks.

"We need to get to LAX and try to grab a flight," said Margot's dad when they'd reached the front of the school, Margot clutching her bag. "Let's go."

"I'll see you in two weeks," said the headmistress with a nod, and Margot stepped into the black car at the curb, letting the dark tint of the windows hide her from the world.

"Margot, wake up. Wake up."

Margot startled awake, blinking uncertainly.

"Where are we?"

"We're at the house."

"Oh."

Sleepily, Margot clambered out of the car that had picked them up from the airport, letting the driver carry her bag inside. They'd ended up having to wait on standby for a flight for hours—so long that Margot had fallen asleep in the airport while they waited to board. Margot followed her dad up the stairs, her dad flicking on the lights ahead of her. The place was so quiet, no noise at all except the rain and the sound of their footsteps. Margot hadn't been here since Christmas—it was strange to be in this space again.

Her dad dropped his briefcase on the floor with a

loud sigh. Margot stood awkwardly at the breakfast counter, tapping her fingers on the granite.

"Dad," she said quietly, "thanks for coming to help me."

Her dad turned to look at her, his brow furrowed.

"Of course I came," he said. "You're my daughter."

"I didn't mean to mess up like this," Margot whispered. Part of her was still upset with him, but there was another part of her that didn't want to be mad at him anymore. "I just want you to know that."

"I just need to make sure you're okay," said her dad, looking her straight in the eyes. "Do you need something else, something other than the deal that we came up with today? I just want you to be happy. I'm willing to do anything to help you make that happen."

Margot considered his words. *A lot will have to change in my life,* she thought. *Is being at this school really the best thing for me?*

"I think I have a lot to think about," said Margot

carefully. And, when she did return to school, she'd have to deal with Grace. Margot was sure the operation would be stopped altogether by the time she got back, but she still had a lot of money to give to them, and she knew they wouldn't leave her alone until she squared up with Grace.

"I'm sorry, Dad," said Margot awkwardly. "For all of this."

"Don't do it again," said her dad grimly.

"I'll try not to, Dad."

He sighed, running his hands through his hair.

"Okay, I'm going to bed. I'll see you in the morning for the first day of your two-week vacation."

"I wouldn't really call it a vacation so much as exile," said Margot. "But, yeah. Good night."

As her dad walked out of the kitchen, he laid his hand on top of Margot's on the counter and squeezed. Margot smiled at him, and for a minute, she was reassured that everything really would be okay.

Chapter Twenty-One

Margot spent a lot of time thinking about her future during her suspension, and trying to get her life back to normal. She talked to her mom on the phone, and it was still hard, but it didn't send her into a spiral of panic the way it had at school, and she considered that a victory. They made plans for Margot to fly out to New Mexico and stay with her for a couple weeks in the summer, and Margot was already starting to look for new clothes for the hot weather.

With Margot's approval, she and her dad and his girlfriend Elsa all went to dinner together, and

Margot was glad to say that it was actually pleasant. It was still hard to see her dad with someone besides her mom, but Margot had to acknowledge that life went on. And she wanted her dad to be happy too.

More and more, Margot also considered what her life would be like outside of Beverly Hills Prep. As much as she loved the campus itself, and some of her classes, she'd never felt like she truly belonged there. And besides Ophelia, she'd never made any real friends, or found anyone she was comfortable around. Maybe it was time to stop wondering what was wrong with her, and instead, change the situation that made her unhappy. Margot began to consider requesting a transfer at the end of the year and finishing her senior year at a school where she could be herself. Maybe she'd even go to New Mexico, for a change of scenery, and to be close to her mom while she finished high school.

"I think it's a great idea," said her dad. "Beverly Hills Prep has never really been a place where you could be happy. And what's most important to me is that you're happy."

While she was showering one morning, Margot realized for the first time how thin she was. Skipping meals due to her anxiety had affected her appetite, and Margot was determined to be healthier from now on. She would have to ask the nurse about that. After she'd showered, Margot made her way into the living room, where, to her surprise, her dad was sitting and watching TV.

"Dad?"

"Hey, kiddo. Look who finally made it out of bed."

"I'm up, I'm up," said Margot. "And, for once, I'm starving."

She managed a full glass of juice, toast, and scrambled eggs, and even more at lunch. They went to dinner at Margot's favorite Vietnamese restaurant together that night, and Margot had an enormous bowl of pho and at least half a pound of dumplings. It was nice to feel normal again, like her old self.

Before she knew it, there were only two days left of her suspension.

"You don't need to stay home tomorrow, Dad," said Margot, as they sat in front of the TV. "I'm just going to pack and hang out. We can do dinner."

"Alright," said her dad. "I'll go into the office tomorrow and then meet you in the evening."

It hadn't been like it was on Christmas break. Not that her dad had stayed home every single day or anything, but he'd been there. He'd made a concerted effort to be there, and it was an effort that Margot wanted to acknowledge with respect of her own.

"Are you feeling ready to go back?" her dad asked.

"Yeah, I think so," said Margot. "I think I'll be able to handle it."

She turned her phone over in her hands; a text had come in from Grace that day:

We need to meet when you get back. Arboretum, three in the afternoon.

Margot couldn't avoid her. There were still a few loose ends that she needed to tie up.

ℝ

The first thing Margot did when she got back to Beverly Hills Prep was sit down with the headmistress for an hour to go over her schedule for the remainder of the year, including counseling times, and earlier curfews.

"I expect you to adhere to this completely, Margot," said the headmistress. "Slipups are not permitted here."

"I understand," Margot said. "And also, Headmistress, I wanted to talk to you about something else, too."

"What is it?"

"I wanted to see what you thought of me transferring somewhere different after this year," said Margot slowly. "I appreciate everything you've done for me, but I'm not sure that I ever really felt at home here.

I'd like to see if there was a different school more suited to who I am where I could finish my senior year."

The headmistress sat back, studying Margot carefully.

"That's a very mature realization, I think, Margot," she said. "I've enjoyed having you here, for the most part, but I tend to agree that I'm not sure you ever really found your niche. The niche you did find was not one I approve of." She looked at Margot sternly.

"I understand," said Margot, flushing.

"I also think you need to focus on your mental health above all, of course. So, if you have a school in mind where you'd like to go, please let me know. I'll make a call or a recommendation to anywhere you'd like to go, once this school year concludes."

"Thank you, Headmistress," said Margot, relieved.

How the tides have turned, thought Margot as they wrapped up the appointment. A whole new life was mapped out for her now. She checked her watch as she stood in the hallway, her heart in her throat. It was time to meet with Grace, and she wasn't sure how she would handle it. Did Grace want to talk to her because she was angry about what had happened? Had something already happened to Kara because of what Margot had told the school? Margot wasn't sure—she hadn't heard anything since she'd been gone. But it was time to find out.

Margot walked to the arboretum and scanned the area for a hidden bench that she knew well; it was camouflaged by an enormous oak tree and set back from the main path. As Margot approached, she saw Grace waiting for her.

"Well, well, well," said Grace as Margot sat down. "Look who's back."

"What do you want, Grace?" said Margot quietly. It was weird being back in Grace's presence—it was so apparent now that she was a toxic person, and Margot was just starting to realize how much so.

Margot was also a lot less intimidated by Grace. She just seemed sort of pathetic to Margot now.

Grace's smile vanished.

"What happened?" Grace said. "Why'd you get pulled out of class that day, and then end up suspended? Kara got in trouble at the last store where we usually get a lot of our stuff, and now she's facing actual charges. The entire operation is on hold, probably forever."

"Look, none of that has anything to do with me," said Margot. "I got pulled out of class because I had a panic attack, and then my dad pulled me out of school for a couple weeks so I could recover. My parents' divorce has been hard on me. That's it. I didn't say anything about you, or Kara, or anyone else. I'm sorry Kara is in trouble, but it has nothing to do with me."

"You still owe us money," Grace retorted, "so even if you didn't say anything, that's still something we need to deal with."

"Oh, right. About that—"

"Where's the money, Margot? Some of the girls I've talked to told me you'd raised prices on your own. What in the world were you doing?"

Margot took a deep breath.

"I started making my own drops," she said.

Grace looked as if she'd been turned to stone.

"What did you just say?"

"That idea that I told you about at the party—I started doing it on my own. I chose drop spots and told the girls where they could pick up their orders, and they left money. I also charged more to show you that it was a good idea, and that you could increase profits."

"I can't believe I'm hearing this."

"I know you guys told me not to do it."

"Yeah, Margot, we did. And you should've listened."

"I'm sorry."

Grace was quiet for another moment, chewing on her lip.

"Do you have cash in those spots, now? Waiting to be picked up?"

"Yeah, I do."

"How much?"

Margot told her, and Grace's eyes went wide.

"Wow," she said quietly. "It looks like your plan wasn't so stupid after all."

"Uh, I guess so." Margot shrugged. She wasn't invested in any of this anymore.

"It worked? Girls left money and made the exchanges without issue?"

"Yeah, all the times I tried it, it worked just fine."

"It is a much bigger distribution zone," Grace muttered to herself. "And girls didn't even seem to care that you'd raised prices."

"No, they didn't care at all."

"Well, Margot, you might have made some really stupid decisions lately, but this one at least proved to be fruitful. By the time everything is cleared up with Kara, we'll have this new plan running seamlessly."

"Wait, what?"

"I think this new system of yours is going to work well with the girls," said Grace.

"Grace, it's over," said Margot. "You said so yourself. This all ends now. I'm out. I'll give you all your money, and then I'm out."

Grace eyed her maliciously, but Margot stood firm. She wouldn't be pressured into any of this ever again. Grace seemed to sense that, as though she could tell just from Margot's tone that she wasn't intimidated by Grace's bluster anymore.

"Fine," said Grace. "Alright, fine."

"Here's a list of all the places you need to look for your money," said Margot, handing Grace the list she'd drawn up. "Everything you need to know is written down on that paper, right there. And that's the last thing I'm doing for you."

Grace eyed her coldly, then looked down and scanned the paper briefly. She seemed satisfied.

"Fine," said Grace carelessly. "You're lucky to get off so easy."

"Whatever, Grace. Have a nice life," Margot said.

She walked away, breathing a sigh of relief that everything was all over.

Chapter Twenty-Two

For the next few weeks, Margot focused on her new life. She went to her counseling appointments, studied and made sure her grades were good, and toed the line. To her surprise, she was enjoying herself. Now that she wasn't trying to make everyone like her, everything was simple. Since she'd removed the stressors from her life, her anxiety had greatly improved, and Margot no longer had to struggle to focus or concentrate. It was a process, and she wasn't a new person overnight, but things were definitely looking up. Grace left her alone, and as far as Margot was concerned, the girl was history. It was harder and harder to understand why she'd ever become affiliated with Grace in the first place, but Margot wanted to let that part of her life go, and not dwell on the past.

Margot began to research schools where she could transfer for her senior year. Her dad was encouraging her to go to one in New Mexico, close to her mom, but there was a small school in Northern California that Margot liked too. With the headmistress's recommendation, it was likely that either one would take her. All Margot had to do was choose.

Now spring was here, and summer was right around the corner. Soon, the seniors would be attending their graduation ceremony, and the year would come to an end. As Margot walked across campus to another class, she tilted her face toward the sun. Beverly Hills Prep might not be perfect, but she would miss it here. Still, it was better for Margot to move on to a different place where she could be herself.

Maybe she'd make some new friends, and maybe

she would love her new school even more than she loved her favorite things about Beverly Hills Prep. All she could do was wait and see what happened— and Margot was perfectly okay doing just that. Instead of being tangled up in problems, she was going to be totally and completely free.

THE END